BOOMERANG DICE

The Complete

Cases of Johnny Hi Gear

STEWART STERLING

---

introduction by Will Murray

illustrations by Arthur Rodman Bowker

cover by Jes Schlaikjer

BLACK MASK
2020

Table of Contents

Introduction

WHEN HE BROKE into *Black Mask* magazine in 1931, Nathaniel Prentice Winchell was one of the most prolific pulp writers of his time. Yet also one of the least known. For his real name never appeared in the pages of any newsstand magazine. In fact, he never used it for any of his fiction.

For his Johnny Hi Gear stories, Winchell called himself Stewart Stirling. This was the first known record of that pseudonym appearing in print. Yet in 1934, *Writer's Digest* claimed that Winchell had been a prolific pulpster since entering the fiction field back in 1925:

> Sterling's real name is Prentiss Winchell. No relation to Walter. Graduating from Dartmouth he put in several years as a newspaper man. Then as an associate editor of Iron Age, adopted pseudonym of Stewart Sterling for his pulp stories, of which he's written more than three hundred, for fifty publications, winning a large following in *Black Mask* with his "Johnny Hi-Gear" series.

None of these pre-1931 pulp stories are known, strangely enough. What pseudonyms disguised Winchell's identity are lost to history. It's possible that his sales included the numerous trade magazines which he edited and to which he contributed. But he used the pen name of Neal Paul Ward in that backwater field.

Even Winchell's full name is cloaked in mystery. In private life and in interviews, he was Prentice Winchell, never once acknowledging his first name of Nathaniel. Many sources cite his preferred spelling as Prentiss.

Stewart Stirling proved to be short-lived as a pen name. Only eight Johnny Hi Gear stories ran in *Black Mask,* beginning with "Boomerang Dice"—all but one appearing between the April 1931 and April 1932 issues. A final installment staggered out in the May 1933 *Black Mask.* "Starita Takes a Rumble" was the title. Then he was gone.

Stirling was part of a wave of fresh blood coming into the magazine with the departure of Dashiell Hammett. Other new writers included Paul Cain, Ed Lybeck and Norvell W. Page, all of whom moved on quickly as well, Page to writing *The Spider,* Lybeck to literary obscurity and Cain—who was really George Sims—to Hollywood.

Despite his modest contributions, Winchell was a member in good standing of "The *Black Mask* Gang." In advance of a 1933 convocation of hard-boiled writers that was to take place at Madison Square Garden during the World Series Rodeo, editor Joseph T. Shaw told one reluctant attendee, "Now, if you don't think the sight of Dashiell Hammett as Don Coyote and 250-pound Prentice Winchell as Sancho Panza, on top of two jackasses, isn't worth the price of a ticket to New York, I miss my guess."

According to Cap Shaw, the cover of the May 1931 issue of *Black Mask* was a portrait of Winchell. In one blurb, Shaw described him as "Six feet and some, 200 pounds and more. One-time life-guard (for fun). Newspaperman, editor, technical writer, yachtsman and general all-around good fellow."

No doubt Prentice Winchell would have remained a regular contributor had it not been for a fluke of fate. For there is no mystery surrounding the disappearance of Stirling and Johnny Hi Gear. What caused them to vanish has been documented.

In 1932, *Black Mask* sponsored a contest for the best radio drama script in the mystery genre. No doubt most of the magazine's star contributors submitted something. Prentice Winchell beat them all.

Yet it was not an auspicious beginning, according to *Writer's Digest*, which reported:

> Sterling... likes to tell about his first rehearsal. Naturally, as he had never been inside a big radio studio before, he didn't intend to miss it. The moment it was over he regretted that he had witnessed it. It seemed to him that cues were being missed with ruthless abandon. Sound effects were all messed up, and the actors had mangled their lines. In shame, he ran off to a corner of the studio, to avoid meeting the director. The director found him out though. He stared at Sterling. He beamed at him, as a matter of fact. "Great work, old man," he commended. "Your program is a cinch. We'll wow 'em!" Sterling looked up at the director, almost speechless from disbelief. He stuttered: "But—but—everything was all wrong." The grin on the director's face became broader than ever. "That's all right," he interposed, "a punk rehearsal always means splendid final performance."

This experience led to Winchell selling scripts to a struggling program called *Eno Crime Club*, sponsored by Eno Salt. This was a pioneering mystery program, which kicked off in 1931. Novels from Doubleday's popular Crime Club series were adapted each week. Someone—either sponsor Eno or syndicator N.W. Ayer—decided that they needed to break free of the constraints of adapting novels to radio.

Winchell's scripting must have been top-notch because when the show moved to NBC in January 1933, he was installed as head writer. Before the year was over, *Crime Club* was renamed *Crime Clues*. For the next three years, under the broadcasting name of Stewart Sterling, Winchell guided the program, writing every script, it is claimed.

Crime Clues was unusual in that the program aired twice-a-week. On Wednesday, the program depicted a criminal case, into which was mixed both aural and oral clues for the audience to catch. This is why the first NBC episode was entitled "Ear Witness."

Listeners had 24 hours to figure out the solution and identify the suspect because on Thursday, Winchell's protagonists, manhunter Spencer Dean and detective Dan Cassidy, stepped in to solve the crime.

This innovative format was a huge hit. Armchair sleuths from coast to coast eagerly listened to the Wednesday night episode, no doubt taking notes as they worked the problem of *who done it?*

Tremendously innovative in its use of pioneering sound effects, *Crime Clues* may have been the first interactive media program ever broadcast. It required the audience to be not mere passive listeners, but active sleuths.

By the time *Crime Clues* had run its course in 1936, Prentice Winchell had soared to become one of the top-rated radio scripters of his era. He went on to write numerous other successful programs, including *The Shadow, Sherlock Holmes, The Saint,* and many others. He once claimed to have turned out more than fifteen hundred radio scripts, and later dabbled in TV and movie writing.

In 1938, Winchell returned to the pulp magazines, again using pen names to disguise his true identity. For *Strange Detective Mysteries,* he called himself Giles Norcroft. That alias lasted only a year.

As Stewart Sterling, Winchell returned to *Black Mask,* but Johnny Hi Gear was not revived. A new editor had replaced Joe Shaw and she was looking for a different type of fiction. For Fanny Ellsworth, he produced three tales centered around racetrack investigator Vince Mallie, all published in 1939.

Thereafter, he took a different approach when Popular Publications bought *Black Mask* in 1940, replacing Ellsworth with Kenneth White.

"When Ken White was editing," Winchell explained, "I originated the Special Squad Series, one novella on specific bureaus in the NYPD; Bomb Squad, Hock Squad, Harbor Squad, etc. That put me in touch with [Police] Commissioner [Arthur William] Wallander and really got me going on the fire marshal series; I spent a lot of time learning why you raise a ladder at right angles to a building, why a man should never straddle a pressurized hose, how to breathe 'from the top' in a smoke-filled room, how to use your feet when opening the door to a roomful of flame.

"Did much of this in department stores for the Don Cadee series; a lot in the Statler Hotel system for the Gil Vine series. Credit Dash for insisting that you have to get your nose in it before you understand it."

Dash was Dashiell Hammett, who turned his experiences as a Pinkerton detective into a career as a crime writer.

This research changed the direction of Winchell's writing career. Going forward, he wrote about realistic investigators, chief among them was Fire Marshall Dan Pedley, who debuted in *Detective Tales* and later starred in ten hardcover novels, all bylined Stewart Sterling.

But he also found time to write the occasional Dan Fowler novel for *G-Man Detective* and the final Black Bat novel, using his Stewart Sterling pseudonym.

Asked the origin of his most famous alias, Winchell explained, "First, I don't want to be confused with Walter Winchell—the lad who snoops to conquer. Second, because I wrote for *Black Mask* and other pulps while I was editor of *The Iron Age,* and the two didn't blend. And last, my wife's maiden name was Sterling—there's a Castle Sterling in Scotland, and Stewart is a Scotch name."

Winchell also revived Spencer Dean, but not as a character. That alias was reserved for his Dan Cadee novels, featuring a security officer working for a famous Fifth Avenue department store.

While he never gained the lasting fame of other *Black Mask* luminaries, Prentice Winchell's career was distinguished. Some forty books were produced. None of them carried his honest byline. Long after he could have broken out as Winchell, he kept his *Black Mask* byline alive.

In 1946, Joseph T. Shaw combed his file of stories he edited that were worth reprinting in his *Hard-Boiled Omnibus* of top *Black Mask* stories. The second Johnny Hi Gear exploit, "Two-Timer," was marked for consideration. But it did not make the final cut.

Back in the 1970s, when I was editing for Odyssey Publications, we brainstormed a *Black Mask* anthology. Among the stories I selected for inclusion was Stirling's "600 to 1." We never pursued the rights seriously, so the project never went forward.

For those who are unfamiliar with the character, Johnny Hiram Gear—to give his full name—worked as under-cover police agent K Five in the earliest years of the Great Depression. His specialty was the gambling racket.

This collection of Stewart Sterling *Black Mask* stories brings together all of Johnny Hi Gear's hard-boiled exploits. None have ever before been reprinted in anthologies. Now they are all between covers, a tribute to an important—but largely forgotten—writer of his time.

Boomerang Dice

Johnny Hi Gear takes a crack at some big ones.

THE FAT MAN in the black sedan was counting bills.

"How'll you have it, Johnny?" he said, sourly.

"Anything but two-spots, Tim." The bronze-faced man in London tailoring turned to look at the board. The numbers for the seventh race were just going up.

"Makes six grand, Johnny. A sweet pick. Ya know somethin'?"

"Hell, no." The broad tweed-covered shoulders shrugged.

"How d'ya guess 'em, big boy? Gotta pipe-line?"

Johnny frowned. He leaned one elbow confidentially on the open window of the sedan:

"Listen, you. I've no inside track. I wouldn't bet a thin dime on these stable tips. And I don't know a damn' thing about horse-flesh either. That'd only cost jack, way they run these hounds in and out. This ain't a race-track; it's a racket."

"Cripes! *You* ain't kickin'? Ya put the finger on four in a row, now."

"No, I'm not kicking. I don't mind playing a game that's framed, long's I *know* it's framed. And I don't have to be wised up on the fix, either. I know hogs, if I don't know horses. That's all these two-timers down here are… a bunch of lousy hogs."

He tucked the roll of yellows in his wallet.

"Give you a chance at it again tomorrow, Tim," he called, strolling away.

"The hell you will," answered the bookie.

A swarthy-skinned individual in a camel's-hair topcoat, with a tan velour fedora to match, jerked a dirty thumbnail in the direction of the departing Johnny, asked a question.

"He's a new one, Tony. A wise one… too damn' wise. Nicked me plenty. Name's Johnny Gear. Just blew in from Saratoga with a wad like a mattress. Why?"

The dark-faced man bit off the end of a panatella, spat it out on the running-board.

"Just curious," he replied.

"Anythin' up your sleeve, Tony? I c'n fix a knockdown, ya wanta meet him."

"Jeeze," said Tony. "What a swell break that would be. A mitt-me from a chiseler like you. No thanks."

Eager-faced men straggled towards the sedan for the payoff. Tony caught up to Johnny at the gate, slapped him heartily on the shoulder.

"Hi, sport," he said.

Steel-gray eyes looked him up, down and through; took in the flashy clothing, the oily skin, the outstretched hand.

"How's tricks?" He had never met this smooth number before, of that he was certain. But when a man goes out of his way to scratch up an acquaintance, well… maybe it wouldn't do any harm to string along a bit and find out why.

White teeth flashed in the swarthy face.

"Just so-so. How you makin' out, Johnny? When I saw you up at the Springs, you were knockin' 'em for a loop."

Johnny was puzzled.

"I've forgotten the name," he said. "Meet a hell of a lot of people, you know."

"Tony Dorio." The Italian was unembarrassed. "Driving in?"

"By taxi."

"Save you the fare, if you like. My bus right around the corner."

As he got into the car, Johnny squeezed his arm against his shoulder-holster.

"Goin' any place special?"

"Dinner somewhere. Why, anything to suggest?" Johnny was anxious to bring matters to a head. What was this egg trying to build up, anyway? If it was a stick-up, Johnny was ready.

"Why not eat with me? Friend of mine runs the Saracen Club. A hot show and swell eats. What say?"

Johnny said yes.

OVER GINGER ALE, cut Scotch and cigars, Tony got down to brass tacks.

"Big boy, you seem to be a regular." Johnny said, "Oh, yeah?"

Tony continued: "There's not so many right guys in this burg, nowadays. Good to meet up with one. How'd you like to make an evening of it? Go places, do things?"

"For instance?"

"Well," Tony appeared to consider. "Buckin' the marbles, say. I can get into a big-time game. A real play with everything on the up an' up. Hear of Constantine?"

Johnny had.

"He's the high spot in this town. A game guy an' a square one, too. Play is a floater… held a different place each night so't there's no protection cut with the flatties and no chance of a shakedown by gorillas. A lot of the real class horns into Connie's game. Billy Devoie, the fair-haired lad in Wall Street; Colonel Harrigan that owns the champs; this Anderton that just cleaned up the pit in Chicago… a lot of the very best."

The fog was clearing up. Some way Tony had found he was flush—seen his roll at the track, probably, thought Johnny. They'd like to ring him in a crooked game and take the roll, would they? Johnny grinned. He knew something about the rollicking dominoes, too.

"Sounds interesting," he said.

They matched for the check. Tony lost.

"Tough," remarked Johnny.

"I'll get it back."

"Maybe so."

They went to Lindy's, asked the cashier for Connie. Connie was out but Tony didn't seem disappointed. As they strolled up Broadway, a car pulled out of the side street, followed them.

The driver leaned out of his seat.

"Lookin' for Connie?" he inquired.

They got in, drove to the Hotel Metropole.

"Room 2410," directed the driver.

They went up. Tony knocked at the door. A stout man in a Tuxedo looked them over.

"Meet Eddie Templar," said Tony. "Mr. Gear's a friend of mine, Eddie. He feels lucky."

The fat man smiled broadly.

" 'T'meetcha," he said. "Don't s'pose I hafta warn ya that Tony here'll take ya back teeth if ya not careful. Ha! Down the end of the hall, Tony." He penciled names on a card, gave it to Dorio. "Suite sixty-seven and nine."

They went down the hall. Dorio knocked twice and slipped the pasteboard under the door.

After a minute, it opened to let them into a small lobby. A thin young man whose mouth twitched unpleasantly put their coats into a bedroom, opened the door to the living-room and resumed his place in the lobby.

Half a dozen men leaned on a long table, covered with green felt. The table had a V-shaped ridge along its center. The air was foul with tobacco and alcohol. A white-haired man with nervous fingers clicked the dice together, rolled them along to the ridge where they tumbled over and came to rest. He did it again. Then he sighed and looked out of the window. Another man took the dice.

Dorio slipped an arm about Johnny's shoulders.

"Want you to know Connie," he said. "Hell of a good guy."

Johnny saw a squat, broad-shouldered man with pasty skin that looked as if it belonged on a corpse, black brows and mustache, high cheek-bones and beady eyes.

"Connie, shake hands with Johnny Gear, a real live one." Tony rubbed his palms together, well pleased with himself.

"Pleasure," said Constantine. "Haven't I heard of you somewhere, Mr. Gear?"

"Maybe. I've been around," Johnny admitted.

"Fellow named Gear almost put the syndicate out of business at Nice last winter. A hunch player, he was. They called him High Gear, if I remember right."

"My father's fault," said Johnny. "Middle name's Hiram. Merely an abbreviation, you see. Nothing to do with my nature. I'm slow going, Mr. Constantine. That roulette story was exaggerated."

"I heard different," replied Constantine. "A drink?"

They had a drink, then another.

"Care to try a pass?" asked the suave Greek.

"Why I came," said Johnny Hi Gear.

JOHNNY DUG IN his wallet, thumbed some yellows.

"Twenty, or any part," he announced.

The Greek's bushy eyebrows lifted a little.

"Mine." He tossed a signed blank check on the cloth.

Johnny shook the dice in his cupped hand, bounced them at the hump. They showed six and five. He made no move to pick up the money.

"It all lays," he stated.

"Right," said Constantine. "You're in the check for twenty. It's good for forty more."

The dice bobbed out again; a double deuce.

"Little Joe's my pal," grinned Johnny.

The dice said nine, three, five, nine, six and four.

Johnny picked up the bills, straightened them out.

"I'm in the check for sixty," he said. "Drag fifty and shoot ten of it. Okey?" he asked.

"Shoot," said the Greek. His voice was flat, his eyes narrowed.

A three and a five showed first, then a six-one.

Johnny said, "Your dice."

Constantine pushed the check with a pudgy finger.

"You've fifty grand in this," he said softly. "Game to go for it all?"

Here it was, thought Johnny. This gambler had no idea of losing a hundred thousand dollars in real money—he knew that. There was a fast one coming, somewhere. He backed away from the table, unbuttoned his coat, eased the shoulder-holster and said.

"Roll 'em."

Constantine rubbed the dice gently between fat palms, tossed them out.

"Eight's my point," he said. Sweat glistened on the pasty forehead.

Someone spoke: "Jeeze, it's hot in here."

"Mix a highball, Tony," said Constantine, rolling a nine.

Dorio held out a tall glass; the Greek drank noisily. He turned to put down the glass and for a second Johnny lost sight of the carefully manicured hands. As the white cubes tumbled out on the green felt, Johnny leaned forward, swept them aside.

"No dice," he remarked.

"What the hell?" Constantine scowled.

"No dice," repeated Johnny. "Player's privilege. No dice. Try a new deck."

The Greek's eyes were pin-points, his voice husky.

"Don't crack wise. These dice are right."

"May be," admitted Johnny. "I just don't like 'em." He stepped clear of the table, made sure there was no one at his back.

"I'm rolling these," growled Constantine. "Try an' stop me." He threw them on the felt.

Before they stopped rolling, they were knocked on the floor by a snub-nosed automatic in Johnny's hand.

"Roll again," he suggested. "If they don't come right, I'll shoot a coupla extra spots in 'em." He waved the gun at the Greek, whose right hand was stealing towards his hip.

"You ———!" snarled Constantine.

"What's the idea of the artillery?"

"Idea is," Johnny explained, "that I don't like to shoot craps with other people's pet dice. Now, fill in that check before this gun goes off and hurts somebody." He tossed something on the table. The Greek stood motionless; the others were silent.

"There's a pen," said Johnny. "You won't have to reach in your pocket. Use it before they have to pack you in ice to keep you from spoiling. *Now!*"

Constantine cursed. On the line where it says: *Pay to the order of*—he penned "Johnny Hi Gear" and swore bitterly as he wrote.

JOHNNY PICKED UP the check.

"This better be good," he said, shoving his right hand and the gun in his coat pocket. "You better be good, too," he added as the Greek edged towards the door. "Stand still."

He backed to the door, opened it and ordered the twitch-mouthed youth to get his coat. He kept an eye on the door until the red light showed at the elevator.

Downstairs, he stopped at the desk for a moment and asked for an envelope. Then he followed a porter through several doors marked "Service," "Danger" and "Baggage Only" to the Employees' Entrance. After looking cautiously up and down the street, he stepped out, strolled uptown.

At the corner of the block he bought a paper. A black limousine stopped at the subway kiosk and a girl stepped out.

Johnny noticed shapely legs and a trim figure, got a glimpse of pert features and blue eyes under the turban.

There was a flurry of skirts, a muffled cry and she stumbled, fell on the curb. He bent down to help her rise. A hand holding a tightly rolled newspaper reached from the car—smacked him solidly behind the ear. He fell heavily beside the girl.

His first conscious act was to damn himself for being taken in by such an old racket. His second was to smile grimly, despite his throbbing head, at Twitch-face sitting beside him in the rear seat of the limousine.

The curtains were drawn and they were rolling along. He heard a ferry whistle below him, noticed that there was no rumble of EL or subway and no jouncing of street-car tracks. He figured he was on the Drive, somewhere near One Hundred and Twenty-fifth Street.

"Wake up, sweetheart," said the hophead, blowing cigarette smoke in his face. "You been asleep long enough. I didn't mean to slap you quite so hard."

Johnny discovered that his hands were tightly tied behind his back. His wrists ached and his temples pounded.

"If you'll just be smart an' loosen up, darlin', we'll take you right home to mama," continued his captor.

"Loosen up?"

"Don't stall. Where's that check? What a fathead you turned out to be. Thinkin' you could walk off with a wad like that. C'mon now. Turn over that check or I'll put a nice pill in your belly. A lead one."

"Too bad," said Johnny. "About that check. Y'see, I had an idea maybe some of you muscle boys would try to get it back. So I left it at the hotel, in the safe. Along with my roll. *Awfully* sorry." He wrenched at his bonds, but they were tightly tied and he only chafed skin off his wrists.

"Is that so?" sneered Twitch-face. "Well, just setcha mind at rest, little one. You ain't goin' t' get off as easy as that. We got ways an' means of makin' guys like you talk pretty. You'll cough up when Connie gets workin' on ya."

"I tell you, I left the check at the hotel."

"That'll just be your hard luck, bozo."

"Yours, too." Johnny turned his head to avoid the foul breath Twitchy blew in his face as he leaned close. "Anything happens to me, jumping-jack, and the house dick at the Metropole will know who to look for. I talked to him, some."

"Cripes!" The dope chuckled. "Ya ain't gotta brain in ya head, have ya? Whadda ya suppose we care what that dumb dick thinks—if he ever does think? He's gettin' graft from Connie regular, anyhow. You'll have me in convulsions in a minute with ya smart ideas."

Johnny thought that he would not care to see his captor in

convulsions if they were any worse than his present affliction. But the dope had mentioned bribing—was there a possibility that way?

"Say, nervous," he suggested. "How'd you like to get a cut of that wad of mine? Take me back to the hotel and I'll see you get it."

"Shut up," snarled Twitchy. "I'll be gettin' a div outta your roll, awright, awright. Not that way, either, weisenheimer. Now, keep ya trap shut. No more gab."

"Says who?"

Johnny tried to duck, but the fist caught him behind the ear. He saw a million stars; fought against the nausea; lost consciousness once more.

HE CAME TO with the shock of cold water. Someone threw another basin-full in his face. He started to get to his feet; discovered he was flat on his back on a cot, ankles roped together and wrists tied on his chest.

Connie put down the basin.

"Feel better?"

"Lousy." Johnny's mouth tasted like rotten eggs. "But well enough to kick the guts out of you, if you take these ropes off."

"So sorry." The pudgy hands spread, deprecatingly. "We've business to attend to first. You understand, I regret all this. But it's your own fault. Did you think you could get away with anything as raw as that?"

"Raw?" echoed Johnny. His ears rang and his voice sounded queer. "Why, you cheap welcher! You're the rawest number I've ever met. If a sucker loses with square bones, fine. If he wins, you ring in those trick dice. If he makes a kick, you beat him up...."

"That'll be all from you." Constantine growled. "Here's paper and a pen. Maybe you'll recognize the pen. You can use your hands enough to write a note to your buddy at the hotel, releasing that check and your roll to my messenger. I'll give you just five minutes." The Greek looked at his wrist-watch, left the room.

Johnny tried to make his throbbing brain work. The chance of escape was slim. The one window was barred, the only other exit was the door by which Constantine had left.

There was no furniture, nothing he could get his hands on. Anyway, if he wrote the note, they would probably wait until they had the dough and then bump him off anyhow. They would be pretty sure to keep him alive until they had the money. They might hurt him some, but if he could hold out until he had a break to make a getaway....

The Greek came into the room with Twitchy.

"The letter?"

"There won't be any letter," replied Johnny.

"No?" The Greek seemed pleased. "You are sure? Nothing could change your mind?"

"Not a damn' thing."

"That's funny," retorted Constantine, sitting on the foot of the bed. "Maybe you're never seen this one?" He took out a gold lighter, flicked it to flame and lit a cigarette. He puffed leisurely, but kept the lighter burning.

"Take off his shoes and stockings." Twitchy did that, got kicked in the belly for his pains and nearly broke Johnny's kneecap with the butt of his gun.

"Sit on his legs," ordered the Greek. Twitchy dug his elbow where it hurt bad, sat on Johnny's legs and grinned. Constantine held the little flame close to the sole of Johnny's foot. At the instep, where it is most sensitive.

"Nice?" he inquired pleasantly.

Beads of sweat rolled off Johnny's face. The veins bulged in his forehead.

"You ———" he managed, gasping.

The Greek tried the other foot. The figure on the cot writhed a little and then was still.

"He's out," said Twitchy.

"Chuck some water on him."

Johnny opened his eyes again. He could not see very well… everything was blurred.

"More?" inquired Constantine, politely, holding the flame under Johnny's toes.

The reply was a groan. The lighter went to the other foot.

"Ah!" moaned Johnny, "You win."

Constantine held a flask to Johnny's lips. Twitchy picked up the pen from the floor, held the paper and looked over his shoulder while he wrote, painfully.

The Greek studied it a minute.

"You better be hoping this works. I don't want to refill my lighter on your account."

But Johnny didn't hear him.

WHEN HE OPENED his eyes, bright sunlight hurt them. Constantine sat on the foot of the cot.

"Thought you were a wise guy," the Greek sneered.

"No," croaked Johnny. His throat was parched.

"Figured you could cross up Tony by sending some trick note, eh? He's been gone four hours. Hear me," he bent close to the cot. "If the bulls get Tony, the morgue gets you. Don't forget it."

"Got me wrong," Johnny husked through cracked lips. "You're dumb as they make 'em. Your sweet little errand boy gave you a runaround. Think he'd pass up a chance to put one over on a grease-ball like you?"

Constantine's face was a dirty yellow as he stared down at Johnny. Then he hurried out of the room. In five minutes he was back, his eyes blazing, his voice trembling with rage.

"So that was it." He smacked Johnny with his fat palm, started a nose-bleed. "Tony got the dough and left two hours ago. He's run out on me. And you fixed it up with him."

"Don't be a sap," mumbled Johnny. "I never saw him after you got that note."

But the Greek was too furious to listen.

"I'm startin' after Tony, now," he shouted. "When I get him...."The pudgy fingers opened and shut significantly. Then he scowled at Johnny.

"But you get yours first." He paused thoughtfully. "You've not been feeling good? Maybe a little ride will help you."

He called to the other room. Twitchy came in, shoved a dirty handkerchief in Johnny's mouth, carried him out into the sunlight to the limousine, threw him in the back seat heavily. A dirty lap-robe hid his bonds from any too curious gaze.

He heard the Greek's voice:

"Take his shoes an' stockings. Maybe he'll need 'em where he's going."

Twitchy laughed.

THE CAR JOLTED along a rough road. At the wheel, Twitchy was mimicking:

"Where shall I take you, sir? The river road, perhaps—or might I suggest Kensico?"

Johnny wracked his brains. He knew where he was going. Some deserted spot where a smash on the skull and a heave into the water would leave no trace of Johnny Hi Gear.

Something had to be done, fast.

The windows might furnish a piece of glass to sever the ropes that tied him, but the sound of a breaking pane would be fatal. If he could only get loose, get behind that hophead, grab the wheel... but there was difficulty in getting to his feet, with the bouncing over ruts and holes in the road. He could squirm and move around under cover of the lap-robe, but what good was that?

"Am I driving carefully enough, sir?" mocked Twitchy. "Or would you care to stop for a bite or a smoke?"

Smoke! That was it. Johnny looked around. Beside him was a little round plug, a length of wire. He leaned back in the corner as if thrown there by the lurching car. He twisted a little, wrenched his arms, caught the lighter with his fingers.

It was only a few seconds before the plug glowed redly, but it seemed an hour. The hot spot bit into the rope. A thin wisp of gray seeped around the edges of the robe and Johnny weaved his body back and forth to dissipate the smoke before it reached the seat ahead.

The car was rocketing now along a concrete highway beside a little stream and the driver had to watch the road.

Johnny winced with pain as he hunched up his knees, fumbled with numb fingers at the knot on his ankles.

The car roared up a steep grade, slowed a bit for a tight curve. Johnny crouched in the seat, tensed his ragged nerves.

There were no cars in sight. Cautiously he opened the door at his right. Twitchy heard and turned.

"What th'—" he began.

But Johnny had leaped for the wheel, jerked it savagely to the left and dived through the open door at the right before the sentence was finished.

He sat up wearily, wiped bloody hands on torn trousers. He touched his sore feet gingerly.

Below him, the limousine hurtled into the air, smashed headlong into a huge boulder, somersaulted and crashed, wheels up, into the stream.

He watched for a minute. There was no sign of life.

He crawled back to the highway, swayed on swollen feet and waited for a passing car.

Finally he flagged a roadster.

IT WAS TWO o'clock when the friendly car dropped him at his hotel. He got to his room somehow, poured out half a tumbler of Scotch, got it inside.

Then he worked the phone for a while.

The house physician came while he was in the shower.

He bandaged the swollen feet without asking too many questions and advised immediate rest.

"Sure thing, doc," agreed Johnny.

He finished shaving while the waiter cut up his steak and poured coffee. He ate slowly, smoked a couple of cigarettes.

The clock in the Club Saracen said "Three" when he walked past the deserted tables to the manager's office.

"Friend of Tony Dorio's," he introduced himself. "Got something important for him. Been trying all day to locate him. Know where I can get in touch with him?"

The manager remembered him.

"You was in with Tony last night," he nodded. "Well, I don't know. If he ain't at the hotel, maybe you can reach him at his girl's flat. He goes there, sometimes."

"Whereabouts?" asked Johnny, and took down an address.

"Thanks," he added. "This means a lot to Tony."

It took a taxi ten minutes to drop him at the apartment house in the seventies. He slipped the switchboard girl a bill and asked questions. Then he used the elevator.

He got off at the fourth floor, was stumped at the closed door. He tried the handle, gently. It turned.

He pushed it open, quietly, standing at one side with his automatic ready. He was looking into a handsomely furnished living-room.

A shadow slowly crossed the patch of sunlight which lay on the blue rug. Johnny took off his shoes, tip-toed softly down the hall. He dropped to hands and knees, shoved the gun around the corner of the door.

"Hold it," he said to the shadow. "Don't even breathe, or I'll plug you." The shadow stopped moving.

HE STOOD UP.

"Well, well, well." He was surprised. "If it isn't my old friend, the grease-ball. What in hell might you be doing here?"

He jabbed the gun in Constantine's fat paunch until the Greek gagged.

"Where's the boy friend?" Johnny asked.

Constantine said nothing but his eyes darted to the door on Johnny's right.

"Turn around. Face the wall. Put your mitts behind your back." Johnny took off his necktie, tied the fat hands tightly.

"Now, you'd have a gun?" he inquired. With one eye watching the closed door, Johnny fished in the Greek's pockets.

He picked out an automatic, an extra clip, three pairs of dice, a familiar wad of yellows and a check to his own order for fifty thousand dollars. All of these, except the dice, he shoved into his coat pocket. The dice he crammed down the back of the fat neck before him.

"You can keep those babies," he said. "They're not so lucky." He poked the gun in the Greek's ribs. "You so much as wiggle and I'll make you ready for a wooden nightie," he said.

He opened the closed door suddenly and looked in.

Dorio was lying on the bed, half-clothed. There was a gaping red wound in his neck and the bed clothes were smeared with blood. A pair of girl's pajamas lay crumpled under the Italian, the pink silk soaking up an ugly red stain.

It made Johnny a little sick to his stomach.

He stepped back into the living-room. The Greek was gone; a bathroom door shut. He put a shoulder to it but the lock held. He put a bullet just below the handle, then another.

It burst open with his next lunge and he nearly fell into the tub.

The medicine chest was open. His necktie lay on the floor, slashed in two with an old fashioned razor that lay beside it. A high narrow window was open. He climbed up, looked out.

Constantine had squeezed his bulk through the tiny opening and made a jump for the fire escape five feet away. His leap was short and he clung by one hand to the metal grid-work. His face was purple.

"Hang on," shouted Johnny. "I'll get you."

He ran into the living-room, opened a window. There was an unpleasant thud from below. He leaned out. The Greek was straddled out like a starfish on the pavement, his neck twisted at a crazy angle.

Johnny lit a cigarette, picked up the phone.

"Get me Spring 2100, sister," he said. "Headquarters? Gimme Inspector Delahan… Delahan? K Five talking…. Yeah! Send over a couple Homicide boys to Apartment 4-C— West Seventy, will you?… Yeah. Two of 'em. Connie the Greek an' a playmate of his… you said it—deader than hell. Report by mail when I get time. S'long."

He hung up.

There was ginger ale in the ice-box and whiskey on the buffet. When they were mixed, he carried the glass to the phone, picked it up again.

"Try Eldorado 6466," he said. "Sure, I'm all right, sister. I just want to get a bet down on the seventh at Belmont."

Two-Timer

Johnny Hi Gear steps with fast company.

THE SHORT-ORDER MAN racked a pile of wet plates, wiped greasy hands on a coffee-stained jacket and craned his thin neck for a better view of the Green Sheet.

"Who's for the third, tomorrah?" He gave up the attempt to read fine print upside down.

The broad-shouldered, bronze-faced man who studied the racing sheet did not lift gray eyes from the columns of figures:

"Havre? Picker says Honey Baby."

"Yah!" The cook slammed a saucer hard on the marble. "That hound. Honey Baby, huh? Cost me a finif las' week. I should go for Honey Baby some more!"

A stocky youth with a pimply face slid back the door, straddled a stool.

" 'Lo, Giff. Gimme a western. Snap it up."

"Howsa kid, Whitey?" The cook broke an egg deftly, tossed a tablespoonful of chopped ham in a bowl, another of onions. "Whatsa rush? You ain't on line tonight?"

"No, dumbell, I'm on a call. Big doin's. Billy-the-Fix gimme plenty sugar to stick around t'night. Soft?"

"Floater, huh?" The cook sliced some bread. "Big shots, huh?"

Whitey grinned.

"Gimme half an' half."

"Hooked a sucker, huh?"

"Said a mouthful. Some mug from Oregon. Senator's son or somethin'. Lousy with dough. Lousy with it."

"Yah!" The cook slid coffee and sandwich down the marble slab. "Papa's l'il man goin' t' play f'r keeps, huh?"

The chauffeur mumbled through a mouthful:

"And *how!* They ring in some talent f'r his benefit, too. A wop. He c'n make a deck sit up an' bark. I jus' been watchin' him at the Metro."

"What the hell? They need that stuff t' take candy f'm th' cradle?"

"No skin off your pants." Whitey wiped his mouth on his sleeve. "An' don' go soundin' off 'bout this party. Somebody'd slap ya down."

"I never open me yap," snorted the cook, resentfully.

Whitey put down two dimes and a nickel.

"So long."

When he had gone, the other customer of Charley's Wagon folded the Green Sheet, stuck it in his pocket and got up.

"Combien?" he asked.

"Scramble two an' large milk, huh? Thirty-five."

The other put down a half dollar, nodded in the direction of the departed Whitey.

"Some sap's headed for a trimming, hey?"

The cook frowned.

"None a my business, brother."

The man with the weather-stained face was halfway down Fiftieth Street before he replied: then the cook could not have heard him say:

"Maybe it's mine."

HE MADE FOR the Metropole cigar-stand.

"Where's those chips?"

"What chips?" The girl behind the case was puzzled.

"Poker chips. I phoned down."

"Oh! 2412? We sent them up. Half an hour ago. I'll find out—"

"Thanks. Never mind. I'll ask the captain."

But he walked past the bell-captain's desk without stopping, made for the elevators. A red-faced Irishman in a derby put a hand on his shoulder. Johnny turned sharply, stumbled over a number twelve shoe.

"Well, well, my ol' pal! Johnny Hi Gear."

Johnny did not look pleased.

"What's on your mind, Tim?"

The detective smiled mirthlessly. "Last time you was in, Johnny, we had a rough-house. Tryin't' start somethin' t'night?"

Johnny shook the hand from his shoulder.

"Keep your paws off. Somebody might think you were putting the bee on me."

"Maybe I will, one of these days."

"I don't think so." Steel-gray eyes bored into the pale blue ones.

"Watch y'r step, wise guy!" growled Tim. "You do any gamblin' 'round here, I'll put you away."

"If you catch me, I'll *go* away and cut out paper dolls. Stick to bill-jumpers and drunks, Tim. They're in your line."

He strolled to a phone booth, grinned at the detective through the glass, spun the dial.

"Inspector Delaney... Delaney? K Five. Yeah. Just a nice game of cards. That's all. Say, what fair-haired lad from the sticks is hitting the high spots now? Politician's son, maybe. Out West. Yeah."

There was a pause. Johnny lighted a cigarette with his right hand.

"Barry Coes? Never heard of him. Well, I'll let you know. Bye."

He hung up, waited until Tim's attention was distracted, ducked behind some palms and climbed casually to the mezzanine.

As he opened the door to the stairwell, he murmured:

"I'll get even with that mick for making me walk up."

Ten minutes later he emerged on the twenty-fourth floor; for another ten he waited until the service car disgorged a waiter with ginger ale, glasses and a bucket of ice.

"2412?" snapped Johnny.

"Yessir."

"Where the hell you been? Hurry it up."

He led the way, knocked on the door.

"Who is it?" squeaked a man's voice.

"Room service," said Johnny. He pushed the waiter forward, stood out of sight at the left.

The door opened a crack.

"Come ahead," said the voice.

The waiter went in. Johnny followed. They were in a small lobby. The door to one of the rooms was open; some men were sitting around a table covered with green cloth.

Johnny closed the outside door. One of the men stood up hastily, kicked back his chair. He had jet-black hair, a pair of shoe-button eyes and a swarthy skin. His right hand was in his coat pocket. He glanced at a fat, bald-headed man in shirt sleeves who held a cigar in one hand, a glass in the other. The fat man breathed very heavily.

Johnny kept his hands in plain sight and said: "Hello Billy. Can't a guy horn into this game without everybody acting unfriendly?"

The swarthy man spoke out of the corner of his mouth:

"Who's th' punk, Billy?"

Billy-the-Fix waved his cigar; his high-pitched voice was apologetic:

"Cripes' sake, Johnny," he squeaked, "somebody mighta plugged ya, crashin' in that way. That ain't smart, bustin' in like that. What's the idea?"

"The idea," Johnny explained, "is poker. I like poker. Heard your driver mention a game, so I came along. That's all. Introduce me to the boys. I know Eddie Templar. How you been, Eddie?"

Eddie said he had been all right. Billy-the-Fix cursed Whitey sullenly.

"What is it? Stud?" Johnny poured out three fingers of rye.

"Draw, you damn' fool. We ain't even started. Couple th' boys 're still in th' next room. You want in? This ain't for love."

Johnny said he never mixed sentiment with business.

THE OTHER DOOR of the suite burst open suddenly; a tall cadaverous individual supporting a pink-cheeked blond youth stumbled into the room. Both were apparently the worse for liquor.

"Meet Fobs Bannock," Eddie Templar performed introductions. Johnny shook the flabby hand of the tall man, a Broadway jeweler with a reputation for not being over-particular about the source of the gems he bought.

"And here," Eddie was jovial, "is Barry Coes, no less. Son of the Senator from Oregon and a regular just the same, even if he *is* a millionaire. One of the best, what I mean."

The blond boy fumbled for Johnny's hand:

"Please ta meetcha," he said, thickly. "Any frien' Eddie's frien' mine."

The swarthy man with the gun in his pocket turned out to be "Paul Vassilo, the baby that furnished the booze."

Paul *might* be a bootlegger today, decided Johnny, but five years ago he had been Vassilo, King-of-the-Deck, and a better sleight-of-hand artist never made Orpheum time.

They sat down. Billy-the-Fix broke the seal of a new deck. Everybody bought chips from Vassilo.

"Play 'em off y'r vest, Barry," warned Eddie, good-naturedly. "This pack 'f wolves 'll take your last dime an' howl f'r more."

The blond boy pulled out a wallet bursting with yellows.

"Sh forty thoushan' bucks ri' here," he boasted, "an' plen'y more where shat came f'om."

Bannock flashed a quick glance at the magician. Billy-the-Fix dimpled:

"Put it away, kid," he squeaked. "Your luck may be runnin', maybe you'll double th' wad t'night. How 'bout it, Johnny?"

Johnny shuffled the cards slowly enough to examine the backs carefully, and said anything might happen.

THE BLOW-OFF CAME about three.

Johnny had been expecting it for an hour and dropped out of all Vassilo's deals. He was a little ahead; the blond boy had lost steadily to Billy-the-Fix. Templar and Bannock were about even with the board.

"Up five yards," said Bannock, Johnny caught a swift glance the jeweler gave Vassilo.

"Jeeze," said the youngster. "There'sh pot headin' my way. Boosht it thoushan'." He fumbled some blues to the center of the table.

"Cryin' out loud, Coes," snarled Vassilo. "You play rough." He shoved in some chips.

Billy-the-Fix looked at his cards and sighed:

"That lets me out, boys. Mine are good, but not that good."

Johnny tossed his cards into the middle of the green felt.

"Guess I'm not in your class," he said.

Templar dropped. Vassilo saw the raise. The jeweler appeared to consider his cards carefully.

"Why not?" he said finally. "Back atcha."

The kid had trouble focusing his eyes on the cards.

"Atta baby," he hiccoughed. "Le's keep out th' shoe clerksh, hey?" He re-raised another thousand.

Vassilo appeared to study the faces of the three who still held cards. Then he shook his head:

"No," he decided. "I'm a sucker to have stayed in the middle as long as this. Out."

The jeweler glanced at the pink cheeks beside him. The boy was leering.

"Whassa matter? Los' ya nerve?" The kid drank the remainder of his highball, turning around to get the glass from a side table.

Bannock stared at Vassilo; the latter's right eyelid quivered. Bannock laughed harshly.

"Come again, kid." He tossed a stack forward carelessly. "'Nother grand."

"'Sa stuff," mumbled the boy. "I'm not yella. Bump 't 'gain."

Bannock paused, uncertain.

"Well, before we get all our dough up, let's draw some cards," he said. "I'll just stay."

The boy grimaced.

"'Me one card," he sneered. "'Sall I need. Jus' one card."

"These suit me," said Bannock shortly.

The boy did not look at his draw, left it lying on the felt.

"'Zhat sho," he mumbled, half rising from his chair. "Think y' c'n shcare me b' shtandin' pat? Nozzir! Can' shcare li'l Barry. Don' care whazza got, c'n beatcha. Got ten thoushan' bucks shays c'n beatcha, n' matter whatcha got."

Bannock's eyes were pin-points of light. He reached into an inside pocket, produced an envelope.

From it he took a sheaf of crisp yellow papers labeled 1000. Carefully he counted out thirty.

"See you," his lips were dry, "an' bump you twenty grand."

The boy looked surprised:

"Twen'y gran'?"

The only sound was the heavy breathing of Billy-the-Fix.

"You heard me," snapped Bannock. "Twenty thou. Cash."

The boy picked up his fifth card, goggled at it.

"Hav'n twen'y thoushan," his voice was blurry. "Eddie, y'r goo' frien' mine? Cash m' check f'r ten thoushan, Eddie?"

Eddie agreed a little reluctantly, helped him make out the check before passing over the bills.

"Lesh go," beamed the youth. "Heresh twen'y thoushan. Watcha got?"

Bannock spread his hand. Three kings, two aces. He reached for nearly eighty thousand dollars....

"Take ya mitts off that dough," snarled a very sober blond young man. "Peek at these."

He spread his cards fanwise, showing four treys, a six.

THERE WAS AN ominous silence.

Then Bannock's chair crashed back. He stared from one to the other of the sneering faces, bewildered. Then he swallowed hard.

"You double-crossing ——— ——— ———," he spat at Vassilo. "You two-timed me, you ———. It's a frame up." His voice rose as he jerked his automatic loose.

Johnny grabbed the bony wrist, brought it up behind the jeweler's back, pushed hard.

"Be nice," he said.

"Pipe down, weisenheimer!" The blond kid hunched forward, one hand on the top button of his vest. His eyes were narrowed, his voice rasping. "Let'm have th' rod."

Billy-the-Fix shoved the blond youngster back.

"Easy, Carl," he squeaked. "Everything's all right."

"Yeah!" The jeweler panted with rage. "Everything's swell. Think you can put that squeeze on me and get away with it?"

Carl—alias Barry Coes—tried to shake loose; the fat man clung to his arm.

"Everything was okey when you figured I was the goat, Bannock," sneered the boy. "Listen, dumbhead. You make one crack about this trimmin', we'll have the story all over Broadway. Laugh that off."

"Take your medicine, Bannock," suggested Vassilo smoothly, "and like it."

The gaunt man glared, his features working convulsively.

"You can't pull that on me," he croaked. "Think I'll let you take me for forty grand? I'll get it back if it's the last thing I do."

"It will be," said Vassilo, "if you try it."

Johnny took cartridges out of Bannock's gun, handed it back.

"You fixed things up pretty," he said to Carl, who eyed Bannock warily. "You look like a Senator's son, at that."

"Aw, shut up," sneered the boy. "What's eatin' you? You're lucky we didn't take you, too. Weaselin' into our game! Hear me?"

Johnny said he heard him.

Bannock backed to the door, his gaze fixed on the hand which Carl kept on the top button of his vest. He reached behind him, opened the door.

Then he walked stiffly forward, raised his arms.

Behind him were two men in raincoats and low-brimmed hats, with masks over their faces. Each held a brace of automatics.

"Up," growled the first. "Keep 'em *high!*"

THE TALL ONE kicked the door to, stood menacingly silent in the little lobby.

"Back up," backed the other, " 'gainst the wall. First mug t' peep gets a load in th' guts."

"Your boys?" whispered Billy-the-Fix to Bannock.

"I wish to hell they were," said the jeweler.

Johnny took the cigarette from his mouth, raised his arms, rested them on the wall.

The short man stuck one automatic in his raincoat pocket and went through Eddie's clothing. He stuffed bills into the raincoat, threw Eddie's gun under the divan.

Vassilo lowered a protesting hand halfway to his waist.

"Nothin' on me," he croaked, "They took me for everything I had."

"Yeah? I'll give ya somethin'." The gunman smashed hard with the butt of his gun. The magician knocked over a chair in falling.

Bannock was next; beside him stood the boy. As the frisker reached him, Carl dropped swiftly to his knees, turned and tugged at his shoulder-holster.

There was a spitting flame, a deafening roar.

Carl mumbled, "What…" through bubbles of blood, pitched on his face.

"Anybody else need a dose?" The masked man kicked the fallen figure savagely.

He stepped in front of Johnny.

"Where's th' wad?"

"Watch pocket," said Johnny.

The killer snarled, jabbed the gun Sharply in Johnny's groin as he extracted the roll from the belt pocket. Johnny grunted.

The knife-like stab of agony doubled him up, brought his right arm halfway down. Beads of sweat rolled down his cheeks.

The stick-up man grinned; Johnny snarled back, held the red tip of his cigarette to the brim of the felt hat above that leering face. The murderer was intent on watching the pain in Johnny's contorted features; even the smell of burning felt was covered up in the acrid pungency of the cartridge smoke.

The other man had slashed the phone cord, half-opened the door. He put out the light. The two backed to the little lobby.

"F'r five minutes," whispered the killer, "the hall will be damn' unhealthy."

AS THE DOOR banged. Johnny jumped for the light-switch, glanced out the window. Several people were on the sidewalks. He grabbed a water pitcher, threw it far out the window.

It burst like a bomb in the middle of the street. Johnny was scrawling on a piece of paper: *"Murder—tell cops guard exits hotel hurry."* He put it in a heavy tumbler, stuck his head outside.

A couple in evening clothes stopped, a little crowd collected. Johnny waved an arm, tossed the glass. The crowd scattered. Someone saw the paper, picked it up. People started running ground like ants.

Whistles shrilled faintly.

Johnny put his head inside.

Bannock was on his knees in a corner, retching. Billy-the-Fix kept moaning: "Oh! My God. A hundred grand. A hundred grand. Oh, my God!"

Eddie Templar was white-faced.

"What'll we do?" he quavered.

Johnny shoved him to the door.

"Get a doc," he said. "Use the floor phone."

He bent over Carl, felt his heart. The boy was dead. The ice-water Johnny threw on Vassilo failed to revive him.

Johnny retrieved his gun from under the couch, put it back in its shoulder-holster. Then he fixed himself a drink.

The doctor came on the run; knelt beside Carl.

"Never knew what hit him," he said, briefly.

"He knew what hit him, all right," replied Johnny. "He was expecting it. How about the other one?"

"Two of 'em?" The doctor's professional poise was broken. "What's been going on?" He worked over Vassilo.

"Stick-up," said Johnny.

"What hit him?" asked the doctor.

"Hard end of a gun." Johnny frowned. "If he's alive, let's get him out of here."

"Stay where you are," growled a heavy voice.

The house detective stood in the door, flanked by two blue-coats.

"Well, well," said Tim. "Been stirrin' things up again, Johnny? What's it all about?"

Johnny told him to go to hell.

"WHAT HAPPENED?" ASKED Tim, while one of the policemen got on a phone in an adjoining room.

"He never had a chance," whined Billy-the-Fix.

"Cleaned us out," muttered Templar, thickly.

"Shut up," yelled the Irishman. "You tell it, boy friend." He waggled a .38 at Johnny.

"Six of us, playing draw," said Johnny, sourly. "Two guys open the door, line us up, take our dough. Carl tried to go for his gun; Vassilo talked back. They got hurt. That's all."

"What'd they look like?" Tim was aggressive; eager on the scent.

"How could we tell, you dope? They wore masks and raincoats. One tall and heavy, the other short and stocky. He was the one used his gun."

The policeman who had been phoning came back.

"Under arrest, all of you," he snapped. "Material witnesses." He took names and addresses, most of them false. "C'mon now. We're goin' over t' th' station. No trouble, I'm warnin' ya."

The house dick helped the doctor get Vassilo on a stretcher, carried him out. The rest put on hats and coats, walked ahead of the bluecoats to the elevator bank.

Somewhere down the hall a door slammed as they turned the corner of the corridor.

"There they are," yelled Johnny. "The killers. Get 'em." He sprinted down the hall. He had no idea the murderers were ahead of him, but what use is an under-cover man who isn't under cover?

As he started, both officers sprang after him; both stopped as suddenly, struck with the same thought; three valuable witnesses would be left unguarded. Then both cursed fervently.

"Stop!" they shouted in unison.

Johnny kept right on.

It took the cops six seconds to snap out of it; Johnny could do the hundred in ten-five.

HE SWUNG OPEN the stairwell door in his stride,

grabbed the Green Sheet from his pocket, folded it into a wad, tossed it down the well. Then he went upstairs three steps at a time.

He opened a steel door, emerged into the cool starlight of the Manhattan night. The clock on the Paramount said four-twenty.

Holding the door ajar, he listened.

A door slammed below.

"Downstairs," said Tim's voice. "There's the paper he was carrying."

Heavy feet pounded down the treads.

"Damn' fool," said Johnny, closing the door.

He made a cat-like inspection of the roof. The penthouse doors and windows were locked. He fiddled at a window-catch with his knife, got it open. Inside, the intermittent glare of an advertising sign three blocks away showed rows of chairs, couches, bolts of cloth.

"Upholstery shop," he chuckled. "What a break!"

He ranged four chairs beside the wall, backs out. A brief tour of inspection brought to light a roll of heavy velour. He removed his coat, collar and tie, hung his hat on a chair and lay down, pulling the thick pile over him.

"Pretty soft," he grinned at the darkness.

When he awoke, the sun was gilding the silver pencil of the Chrysler Tower. He was stiff, his mouth dry. He found a wash-bowl, soaked his head in cold water, drank deeply.

Beside the washbowl was a row of lockers. He could not get them open, though he wasted several minutes trying. As a last chance, he reached on tip-toe, felt on top.

He dragged down a pair of brown overalls, covered with dust.

He put them on, looked in the mirror. Without collar and necktie, hatless and with a day's growth of beard, he looked very unlike the debonair gentleman of the previous evening. A smudge of dirt on his chin further helped out the makeup.

The coat, collar and tie and hat he rolled into a bundle, wrapped them in a piece of scarlet damask. This he put on a freshly finished chair and carried chair and bundle downstairs.

An elderly maid in a fresh gray uniform was just closing the door to 2408.

"Chair for 2408," said Johnny in a bored voice. "Open up, will ya. I ain't got all day."

She grunted something unintelligible, unlocked the door. He carried the chair and bundle inside, shut the door. The chair went in a corner, the scarlet damask in the closet.

First he phoned for ham and eggs, coffee and rolls. After breakfast he picked up the phone.

"Is the men's shop open yet?" he asked the operator.

"Yessir. Just a minute."

"Metropole Men's Shop."

"Say," said Johnny, "I need a new hat. Some son of a gun burned mine with a cigar last night. Send up two or three for me to make a selection, will you?"

He gave his head size and room number, said he thought brown would do for color, hung up.

Presently there was a knock on the door.

"C'min," said Johnny without rising.

"Morning, sir," said the clerk. He set down four hatboxes.

"Let's see," Johnny got up. "I suppose this will cost me ten bucks, but I'll get it back, see if I don't."

The clerk grinned sympathetically.

"Must have been quite a party," he said, " 'nother fellow had a hole in his lid this morning, too."

"Ah," said Johnny. "Who was that? Tommy Baker, eh?"

"No, sir. Mister Switzger, his name was. I forget his room. Twenty-third floor, I think. Hole burned right through the brim."

"Tough," said Johnny. "I'll take the Borsalino."

"Thank you, sir."

The clerk went out. Johnny didn't wait to take off the hat before reaching for the phone.

"Hotel information," he said. He lit a cigarette. "Can you give me Mr. Switzger's room number, please?"

HE TOOK OFF coat, collar and tie, put on the overalls again. Then he carried the chair and bundle one flight down. He knocked at the door of 2364. There was no answer. He knocked again, waited a minute.

He carried the chair around to the floor-clerk's desk.

"Chair for 2364," he said.

The white-haired woman on duty glanced at him briefly.

"Maid'll let you in," she said. "Okey, Agnes." A dark-haired slip of a girl walked in front of him to the door, unlocked it. He went inside.

He set the chair down, closed the door. In the wastebasket was an old felt hat with a hole in the brim. A cowhide suitcase stood on the rack.

On the dresser was a taxi-license. The photograph was that of the pimply-faced youth called Whitey, but the name under it was John Rakewski. Beside it was an application for a revolver-permit made out by J. Rakewski and endorsed by Wm. Wilson.

"I never heard Billy-the-Fix called William," chuckled Johnny.

He opened the bathroom door, looked in. A hand came out from behind the shower-curtains, with a blackjack. He started to duck, there was a burst of white light, his knees buckled.

When he came to, he was choking. The air was suffocating; he was in absolute darkness. He was not tied or bound, but his back was against one wall, his head jammed into another.

It took him a minute to realize that he had been thrown into a closet. His gun was missing, cigarettes and matches gone.

He sat up, his knees under him. There was the sound of a key in a lock, feet passed his door. There was no keyhole through which he might see. He stood up shakily.

A raincoat brushed his face. He pushed it away, felt something heavy in the pocket. His hands fumbled around in the darkness. He grinned twistedly as he got his hands on the gun which the murderer had left there after the holdup.

There were voices outside. He held the gun in readiness, slipped back the catch.

"My God! Don't do that. Don't—"

He heard a muffled explosion, a falling body. Then the door slammed.

He held the automatic to the lock. Four shots it took to smash it. The door fell open and he stumbled into the room, choking with the acrid fumes of powder.

Light hit his eyes like a physical blow. He blinked at the figure on the carpet, a short, stock man lying face down. There was a dark stain that looked like water by his left side.

He turned the body over. Whitey, the taxicab driver, had a hole through the upper left-hand pocket of his vest. It was a matter of seconds for Johnny to get into the hall. He saw a door swing at the end of the hall, made for the stairwell.

His knees felt like water and he had to grip the banisters tightly to keep his feet as he went down one flight. He opened the door to the twenty-second floor. A gun jabbed into the pit of his stomach so suddenly that he gagged.

"Put up ya mitts," came a growl from the other side of the door.

Johnny raised his hands.

"Stick 'em out here," said the voice.

He put his wrists through the open door. There was a cold touch of steel, a click and the handcuffs were on.

The door swung wide.

"Well, well," said Tim Finkler, "see what I found. There's a bull downstairs lookin' for you, Johnny."

Johnny felt too sick to say anything.

THEY WALKED TO the floor-clerk's desk where Tim used the phone.

"That bird is back," he said jovially, after a little wait. "Better come up an' put him in the cage."

Johnny leaned against the wall, fought off nausea until a plain-clothes man and a bluecoat got off the elevator.

"Much obliged, Tim," said the Central Office man. "We'll take care of this baby for you." He turned to Johnny. "What the hell? Where did you go last night? And what good did it do you?"

"Hello, Myers," said Johnny wearily. "I went places and found things."

"Such as?" Tim asked the question.

"A dead man upstairs," said Johnny.

"Who?" Myers was startled.

"Where?" inquired the policeman.

"I'll show you, if you'll let me."

"Lead the way, fella. If you know what's good for you there won't be any more tries at a getaway. I'll give you the heat next time."

Johnny climbed the stairs painfully, walked to 2364, waited while Tim used his pass-key.

Myers looked at the body.

"Whitey Rakewski," he said. "What you know about that?"

"What's it all about?" the policeman was puzzled.

Tim said nothing; kept a sharp watch on Johnny.

"Whitey did the killing upstairs last night," explained Johnny. "His partner, double-crossed him and knocked him off. I suppose he didn't want to split the dough, or else he was afraid of a squeal. Anyway, he killed him."

"How come you know so much about it?" snarled Tim.

"I was in the closet," replied Johnny. He told his story tersely.

"You're a damned liar," shouted Tim. "You bumped him yourself. I think you was in on the stick-up, too, anybody asks me."

"Nobody asked you," said Johnny, wearily.

"He's only been dead a few minutes," said the detective. "He's still warm."

"I caught this punk running downstairs," glared Tim.

"Looks bad for you." The cop poked Johnny in the ribs with his stick.

Tim stood in front of him, hands on hips.

"Better come clean, kid," he said.

"Why me?" asked Johnny.

"Who else?" snapped Myers.

Johnny held out his manacled wrists.

"There's the killer," he said, pointing at Tim.

THE PLAIN-CLOTHES MAN stared blankly. Tim swung for Johnny's jaw.

"You ——— ———!" he snarled.

Johnny took the blow glancing, kicked hard. Tim grunted and fell back across the bed, holding his belly.

"You'll find the dough on him," said Johnny. "There'll be a couple of thousand that are mine. The bills are marked."

"You're crazy," said the Central Office man. "You can't pin this on anyone else."

"He killed Whitey," added Johnny. "The bullet will have marks of his gun. Better get it before he starts to use it."

Tim lost his head.

"Is *that so!*" he said hoarsely, getting to his feet. "I'll show you who killed Whitey." He pulled out his automatic, fired at Johnny. The policeman knocked up his arm, grabbed the gun. The bullet chipped plaster from the ceiling.

"Lay off," barked Myers. "No rough stuff, Tim. Gimme your rod."

Tim lashed out with his fists, kicked and used his teeth. He got a smash behind the ear for his pains, fell on his face.

"When I got in the room," Johnny explained, "somebody clipped me one and threw me in the closet. That was Whitey. Then Tim comes in and gives the works to Whitey while I'm in the closet. I find a gun that Whitey's been careless enough to leave in a coat, bust the lock and chase along. Then Tim doubles back, puts the bracelets on me."

"How'd you suspect Tim?"

Johnny smiled.

"His shoe," he said. "I stepped on his shoe downstairs in the lobby earlier in the evening. When these stick-up gees come in, I had a flash at their feet because that was all I could see. There's a heel mark on Tim's right shoe still." He pointed to the circular mark on the polished box toe of the Irishman's number twelve.

"I dropped a note out the window. The exits were all guarded before the stick-up men could get out, and no one tried to get out. Then it all fitted in," continued Johnny, inhaling leisurely. "Tim could enter the rooms easily with pass-keys. He was about the height of the taller gunman and he didn't talk because he was afraid I would recognize his voice."

The house dick shook his head and opened his eyes.

"Self-defense," he mumbled. "Whitey tried to get me first."

"Bull," said Johnny calmly. "You knocked him off for the dough. If it were self-defense, he'd have half the coin on him."

"That's right," said Myers. "Well, let's go. You nearly pulled a fast one on me, Finkler. You'll find it tough to talk your way out of this, though." He jerked the Irishman to his feet.

"You better come along, Johnny," he added, apologetically. "Material witness, you know. You can get bail."

"Bail, hell," said Johnny. "What I need is a drink."

Cold Blood

*Johnny Hi Gear, fast-stepper, has to move
fast to keep ahead of this trouble*

THE HEAVY-SET MAN shoved his derby back on a low forehead, spat casually on the floor and squinted at the three cards in the widow:

"Gravy," he grunted. "King makes eighty kings an' jack gimme forty pinochle. Meld a hundred sixty, two forty, two sixty, three hundred. I sink thirty... so...."

At his left a thin, silver-haired individual with a white dickey and shiny *pince-nez* set on a high-bridged nose, tossed his cards down as if disgusted.

The tall, wide-shouldered player at his right adjusted the brim of a soft felt over a bronzed face, placed his cards carefully in the middle of the table and stood up.

"That washes me up, Spigler," he said. "Owe you fifty cents. And maybe, an apology."

The big man scowled suspiciously.

"For what?"

"For calling one of you birds a cheap chiseler."

There was an ominous silence. The thin man kicked back his chair, stood up warily.

"What you mean?" he whispered.

"One of you guys can't even play a lousy little ten-cent game without remembering he's a crook. This deck's spotted." Johnny Hi Gear picked a dozen cards out of the pack, flipped them face down. He shuffled them around, picked out five.

"Aces," he said. "Touch of booze on one edge—the alky takes

off enough ink to spot the card any time. I've been reading them for an hour."

He selected three other cards.

"Should be kings," he announced. He turned them over: two spade kings, one heart king. "A small spot in the corner, for kings."

The heavy-built man lumbered slowly to his feet.

"You think...?"

"Don't kid me. I *know*. I don't care about a few bucks, but I hate to be taken like some dumb bunny of a sucker. I don't know which of you did it; maybe both. The deck was clean when we began. One of you...."

The silver-haired man snarled, grabbed a ginger ale bottle. But the big man struck first. Johnny ducked, clipped a hook to his stubbly blue chin. The bottle smashed down.

He took it on the shoulder, swung again for that unshaven chin. A pair of sinewy arms grabbed him, spoiled the punch. Spigler bored in, an ugly grin on his oily face, a savage look in his shoe-button eyes.

Johnny took a glancing blow on the forehead and got in a jab with his left.

Spigler grunted, fell backwards over a chair and crashed in a heap in the corner, his head in a brass cuspidor.

The thin man clawed and scratched at Johnny's face, hanging on his back. Johnny dropped to his knees, catapulting the other over his head. There was a squeal of fright, a sound of splintering glasses and a crash that could have been heard on Broadway.

Johnny got to his feet, felt of his face, brushed his pants.

"What th' hell?" A very fat man with a double chin, baby blue eyes and a disarming dimple, stood staring in the doorway. "What's goin' on, huh? You sure must like rough-house, Johnny. Never see a gee like you f'r gettin' in a mix."

He walked into the room and the baby blue eyes widened:

"Jeeze! Know these babies?"

Johnny straightened his necktie:

"Can't say I care to, Billy."

Billy-the-Fix dimpled.

"You prob'ly will, just th' same. They'll be lookin' you up, one 'f these days. You better see 'em comin'."

Johnny grinned and said he slept with his eyes open.

"THE BIG GUY is Uncle Benny Spigler, a sort of, uh, pawnbroker, know what I mean?"

"I can guess."

"The other," Billy-the-Fix said, as they walked past the bowling alleys, pool tables and slot machines, "is Solly Wagman. My lawyer. A damn' good lawyer, too. C'min th' office a minute."

"This your place, Billy?"

"One of 'em." The fat man opened a door marked:

Claridge Bowling & Billiard Parlors
W. Wilson, Mgr.

He sat down in a rickety swivel-chair before a roll-top, produced a bottle and some glasses.

"Have a shot? Good stuff."

"Mind if I do. Thanks."

"Solly," continued Billy-the-Fix after the glasses were refilled, "is so damn' wise I got to watch my step pretty close. He's too slick even for a lawyer. And he's tough. Don't forget it."

Johnny drank the Scotch.

"Good booze," he admitted.

"F'r that matter, Uncle Ben is no playmate f'r babies. He'd steal the fillings out of a stiff's mouth. How'd you mix with those boys, huh?"

"Pinochle. Marked deck."

"Which one?"

"Hard to say. Either might have. They both took a punch at me; your friend Solly tried to crown me with a bottle. So I talk back. That's all." Johnny lit a cigarette.

"Um. I'll say it's all, f'r a while. You know how to handle y'self in a jam, Johnny. You sure do. Want a job?"

"Such as?"

Billy looked at the ceiling.

"I carry around a lot of dough. Have to, in my line. You know how it is." Johnny nodded.

"Then my rocks." He fingered the enormous solitaire which blazed on his left hand. "They're worth quite a bit, huh?"

"Well? Where do I come in?"

"Right there, Johnny. Seein' no wise boys fan me for th' roll. And the rocks."

"What's wrong with Eddie Templar?" Johnny's face showed no more interest than if the other had asked for a match. "Thought he was Man Friday?"

The fat man coughed, apologetically.

"Eddie's oke," he said. "But I could use you, too. Ya got nerve an' guts. Well, Eddie's got those. But brains, now. Eddie has t' have me do his dome-work for'm."

Johnny flipped his butt out the window.

"You got me wrong, Billy. I'm a gambler, not a muscle-boy."

"Jeeze!" The fat man's voice rose shrilly. "Ya ain't even heard th' proposition yet. Siddown a sec'."

"You couldn't hire me as bodyguard, Billy. You ought to know better than to try."

"For a thousand a week?"

Johnny looked impressed.

"You must be scared as hell, Billy. Who's been frightening angel child, so's he'll loosen up for a grand?"

There was a sharp knock on the door. Johnny got to his feet as the door opened. A stout, red-faced man with a cigar stuck aggressively in the corner of his mouth, said: "Hello."

"Hi, Eddie. How're tricks?"

"So-so. How you been, Johnny?"

"Keepin' out of trouble, that's all."

Billy-the-Fix laughed nervously.

"Yeah. A scrap a day keeps th' doc away. See anybody on ya way in, Eddie?"

"I was just goin' t' tell ya," said Eddie Templar. "That mug

Spigler's standing in a dark corner 'f th' hall, downstairs, waitin' f'r somebody. I made out I never see 'im. What's up, boss?"

The fat man laughed again, more nervously than before.

"Ask Johnny," he squeaked, and to Johnny's alert ears, his voice held a note of fear.

Templar looked the question.

"I think Mister Spigler"—Johnny got up—"has a date with a punch in the nose."

"Watch ya step, big boy," Billy called after him, with an attempt to be jocular.

"I'll do that," said Johnny.

AS HE WALKED past the darkened bowling alleys, he grinned, stuck his thumbs and fingers in the grip-holes of two of the heavy wooden balls. Swinging them slightly, he kicked open the door and walked softly to the head of the stairs.

He listened. The staircase was lighted by a dim, fly-specked bulb, but the hall below was dark. And silent.

He crept quietly halfway down, leaned over the banister, swung his right hand out and back.

There was a sudden exclamation, the thud of something heavy striking something soft and the dull bump as the ball hit the floor.

Johnny transferred the other ball to his right thumb and middle finger, swung it out and over.

A stream of obscenity came hoarsely from below. Somebody had taken that missile where it hurt. There was a sound of running feet, a door slammed.

"Good night, Benny," murmured Johnny as he got to the street level. There was no answer—he didn't expect any.

He opened the glass door, checked himself in the act of stepping to the sidewalk. In the mirror-like surface of the door he saw the reflection of a figure standing across the sidewalk and outside his direct line of vision. The face of Solly Wagman was distorted with rage; that much he could see in the impromptu glass.

He closed the door, stepped back in the shadows. He had managed to drive Spigler away by an unexpected attack with the bowling balls, but this was something different. He didn't feel in the mood to act as target for a slug; he didn't care much about messing up in a gutter-brawl with its attendant newspaper publicity.

He considered, smoked a cigarette. Spigler had beat it, but not out the front door. Well, then, he'd find that same exit Spigler had used and drift out without any noise or fuss with Wagman. Maybe he'd cool off, over night.

There were noises above: moving feet. He drew back into the corner Spigler had occupied, kicked a big round object out of the way and waited.

The feet sounded through the door and down the stairs.

There were two men and they moved cautiously. They were Billy-the-Fix and his bodyguard Templar.

They went out on the street. Johnny hesitated only a second and followed. They were at Thirty-ninth Street, going north. Half a block behind them trailed Sol Wagman.

Johnny pondered many things as he started after them. Why the sudden rush? Perhaps Spigler hadn't trailed him to Billy's. Perhaps his business was with Billy instead. And why was Wagman waiting outside when he was sure of entrance to his client's? Or a telephone message might have come in that had nothing to do with either Spigler or Wagman.

Johnny didn't have the answers, so he joined the procession. It led to the subway kiosk at Fortieth. They were on the platform when the train rolled in, a Broadway-Van Cortlandt local. Johnny had no nickels; he tossed half a dollar at the coin-change man, shouted: "Keep the change," and vaulted the turnstiles.

He made the train by shoving a guard out of the way.

He worked his way back, one car at a stop. At Sixty-sixth he saw Eddie Templar talking excitedly to Billy-the-Fix in the middle of the fifth coach from the rear.

Eddie kept his right hand in his coat pocket as they switched to the express at Seventy-second. Johnny changed, too.

"Must have been in a hell of a rush," Johnny said to himself, "Couldn't wait for the express at Times Square. Who are they ducking from, I wonder." For he had seen no one resembling Sol Wagman at Seventy-second—and he had watched carefully.

At Ninety-sixth the local stops between express and local platforms; if the doors open right, an alert man can step off the express, cross the platform, walk through the local to the exit.

But Johnny watched his men sit quietly while the express emptied and filled again. A local pulled in. The express doors started to close. As they slid back Eddie dived, caught the rubber guard and the door automatically opened again. They sprinted across the platform into the local train.

Johnny cursed. The door to his coach had closed a few seconds before the others; the train was under way, pulling out. He stepped into the space between the cars, got his foot on the guard chain and jumped. He sprawled on the platform as the express roared out and someone shouted at him.

The local was also on the move. He had to gamble, then. If they had taken the local he was licked—and he wanted to know what this midnight excursion was all about.

He got to the street, looked around. No sign of Billy or Templar or Wagman. Was that somebody running down Ninety-sixth towards Riverside, towards the viaduct?

He took a chance. The running figures came into clearer view as he put everything he had into a sprint. He almost lost them again when they darted south into the vaguely lighted section south and west of the tracks.

He was fifty yards to the rear when they disappeared. He slowed up, walked cautiously until he came to a big gate on which was painted

STUYVESANT YACHT CLUB
Members Only

The gate was locked, the clubhouse dark. A high board fence surrounded the club. Billy had used a key, then.

The faint rattle of oar-locks came to his ears. He put an eye to a crack. A dinghy was pulling out towards a big cruiser moored on the outer line.

Johnny waited through long, silent minutes, his curiosity unappeased. He had seen Billy-the-Fix not so long ago in a fast game in which hold-up and murder had had a part. He wanted to learn the reason for this sudden hideaway.

He listened vainly for sound of the cruiser's engine; and after a time heard the faint noise of returning oar-locks. When this ceased, he waited another minute and then decided to go into action.

Johnny ran back ten feet, came in fast, leaped high and caught the top boards. The fence swayed and creaked under his weight: he dropped into the blackness on the other side.

Johnny found a flat-bottomed boat upturned on the float; got it in the water.

A squeak of dry leather startled him. He glanced up, heard a grunt, tried to dodge the blur of downward motion. His senses exploded in a blinding flare of light and pain.

His body was rolled to the edge of the float, flopped into the river.

The tide swept him swiftly upstream, and out.

THE HUDSON IS ice-water in April, so the chilling shock partially revived him. But it was the violent smash with which his face collided with a round, cold, hard something that made him open his eyes.

Subconsciously he put up a hand to protect nose and mouth from the battering; his fingers caught a slimy cable. He spat out a mouthful of bloody salt water, hung on grimly. For long minutes he gripped the mooring buoy while stars whirled crazily overhead and shore lights danced dizzily on the black water.

Near at hand, as his eyes came into focus, he saw the blaze of lights from the ports of a sixty-footer. He was nearer that warm light than the vague and distant shore line. Painfully he stripped off his coat; tried to loosen his leaden shoes; failed.

His muscles ached miserably with cramps; his head was splitting but he let himself go, struck out for the cruiser.

For weary hours, it seemed to him, he battled the tide until he touched a white stern bearing big bronze letters reading

Jingler. The name sounded familiar and he tried to remember, but his brain refused to work. Right now his need was for rest and warmth.

He shouted. Not even an echo answered.

He got a hold on an exhaust pipe at the water line. It seemed hopeless. There was nothing he could reach to pull himself up; the *Jingler* had high free-board. His legs were getting numb from the freezing flood.

"Got to make it," he chattered through rattling teeth. "I'm through, unless I make it."

He saw that the cruiser was held only by her forward mooring line, and of course her stern swung away with the run of the tide.

The smooth side offered him little assistance in his battle against the current to reach the bow and the slanting, slimy cable.

Ever try to get aboard that way—when you felt husky and were not exhausted—at the start?

With veins standing out on his forehead and eyes starting from their sockets, Johnny dragged himself free of the water, gained the bow after prodigious effort and with a mighty heave pulled his body up and across. Then he fainted.

When he came out of it, the *Jingler* was wrapped in a cotton-wool fog. He shivered, stumbled to his feet, fell again. On hands and knees he crawled off to the deckhouse.

"Hello!" he called. No answer. He staggered down the aft-companionway.

Billy-the-Fix was sprawled over the starboard bunk, legs limp, head sagged on his chest.

JOHNNY TURNED HIM over. There was a black bruise on the fat man's temple; his skin was bluish-white. But he breathed. Slow, halting gasps they were, but breath.

He fished cigarettes from Billy's pockets, lighted up. Then he broke open a locker, found a bottle of whiskey.

He drank deep, coughed as it burned his throat. Then he peeled off his soaking clothes, rubbed himself raw with a towel, put on a bathrobe he found in the locker.

A third stiff jolt from the bottle pepped him up a bit. He went forward. The bow stateroom was a shambles. The door mirror was broken, cushions torn, papers scattered on the berths. Drawers had been smashed in. There were brown stains on the blankets. A black stream trickled beneath the lavatory door. Inside he found what was left of Eddie Templar.

The bodyguard had a dozen knife stabs in chest and stomach; his neck was slashed; blood from his wounds had drenched his clothing.

Johnny looked at the glazed eyes and shivered.

Save for the corpse and the unconscious man, the *Jingler* was deserted. He already knew the dinghy was gone.

In a forward closet he found a suit of clothes, shirt and cap. He took them to the deckhouse.

In the after cabin he got another drink inside him and sat down opposite the fat man.

Eddie murdered—where was the knife? Billy knocked cold by bad booze, or what? They came out in a dinghy—where was it? Who had cracked him on the head, back there in the darkness? Why should Billy-the-Fix, smart a schemer as ever was, get Eddie on board this yacht just to cut him up, when he could have done it much more quietly ashore? Why the search in the forward stateroom, as shown by open drawers and scattered papers?

"It's all wrong," he mumbled to the limp form opposite. He bent over, propped the fat figure to a sitting position. A clenched right hand, previously hidden by his body, flopped into view. Johnny stared, not at the huge solitaire, but at the hunting knife which fell from the fat fingers.

There was a stain on the blade, red on the handle. The palm that gripped the knife was smeared a sinister brown.

He chafed the fat wrists, slapped the plump cheeks so that the bald head rolled from side to side, forced whiskey between the flabby blue lips. He put a wet towel back of the thick neck, stuck a pin into the fleshy leg. The pale blue eyes didn't open.

"Billy, you and me are in a jam. First, I have to get clear, myself. Then, maybe, I can do something about you. But," he addressed the unconscious man confidentially, "if I thought you did that... in cold blood, I'd chuck you in the river right now. I don't think you did."

Carefully he went through Billy's pockets. The wallet was gone; there were no papers in the coat pocket. He wore a money belt. It was empty.

"That was dumb," commented Johnny cheerfully. "Man doesn't commit murder to rob himself. Billy, what in hell was this guy looking for?"

Crumpled in a corner was a gray fedora. He opened the sweatband. Nothing there. He ran a finger around behind the black silk hatband. He felt a piece of pasteboard, brought it to the light.

It was a pawn-ticket for a diamond ring, redemption value $2,500. *B. Spigler* was printed on the slip.

Johnny thought he began to see light. He slid the ring off the plump finger, put it with the ticket in a vest pocket of the suit on the deckhouse floor. Then, with a towel, he went carefully over rails, hatches, stanchions and door knobs for fingerprints he might have left. He didn't touch the smashed drawers.

An oilskin went around the suit, shirt and cap. With his belt, he strapped the bundle to a life-preserver. Then he tied his shoes together by the laces, knotted them to the bundle on the canvas ring. As a last thought, he took off the bathrobe, added it to the pile on the preserver. Carefully he dropped the whole outfit overside, dived in after it.

The tide was slack and, free from cumbersome clothing, he made the float easily. He rubbed down with the bathrobe, put on the dry clothes and wet shoes, cursed as he pulled the cap over the bump on his head.

A cold gray lightened the darkness over the apartment on the Drive as he climbed towards Broadway.

A TAXI TO the Metropole; ham and rolls and coffee, plus a red-hot bath and two hours' sleep, set him up considerably, although his head pounded, his ears rang and every muscle ached like a sore tooth. There was a patch of skin missing from his chin where he had banged the mooring and his shins were black and blue. But he grinned at his reflection in the shaving mirror.

A fresh suit, new shoes and his old black felt and he was set to go. He took the elevator, got to a booth and fiddled with the dial. Presently he crossed Fiftieth to Broadway and stepped into the jewelry store on the corner.

"Nice day." He grinned at the gaunt man behind the ring-counter.

"What of it?" Fobs Bannock didn't sound friendly.

Johnny produced the ring, rubbed it on his sleeve.

"Ever seen this?"

"I'll say." Bannock laughed unpleasantly.

"What's it worth?"

"Say, five hundred."

"This stone? What the hell you mean?"

"I'm telling you." The jeweler leaned confidential elbows on the counter. "And I oughta know. I made it."

"Phoney?"

"One of the best." Bannock grimaced at the thought of the fat man who had framed him in a poker game. "Billy Wilson prob'ly told you it was the McCoy. I made that glitter coupla years ago, f'r him."

"Go on."

"Well, it's a double. The real one is prob'ly in hock. He usually sticks it on ice when he needs cash. Good stone, too."

Johnny put the ring in his vest pocket.

"Thanks a lot."

Bannock frowned.

"Say, how in hell d'ju get that? That pot-bellied ——— sell it to you?"

Johnny said it was loaned, temporarily.

At the corner of Forty-sixth and Seventh he stopped before a window full of rings, watches and cameras.

He went in. Spigler was in the wicket at the rear. He glared at Johnny.

"You got a nerve," he growled.

Johnny pushed the ticket across the shelf.

"My ———!" Spigler's face was ashen.

"What's trouble?"

"Where'd you get that ticket?"

"That's my business. Where's the ring?"

The pawnbroker looked stupefied.

"Oh! In the safe. Can't get it out now. In an hour. Come back in an hour. I'll have it for you."

Johnny looked at him steadily.

"You better," he said.

FIVE MINUTES IN warm spring sunshine brought him to the Bar Building on Forty-fourth. He got off the elevator at the third floor, located the door lettered *Solomon Wagman, Attorney.*

In the waiting room, he gave his name to a blonde at the desk, was ushered into a private office that gave no evidence of springtime. The windows were shuttered and heavily curtained and electric lights were burning. Evidently Solly had need of extreme privacy, thought Johnny.

He didn't offer to shake hands with the lawyer.

"Eddie Templar was bumped," he began.

The attorney's grimace of dislike at the man who had beaten him the day before swiftly changed to an expression of surprise.

"What's that?"

"I said Eddie was morgue meat. Butchered. On the *Jingler.* Last night."

"Cripes—"

"What I came about was this." Johnny laid the solitaire on the desk. It seemed to fascinate the lawyer.

"Where'd you get hold of that? It's Billy's."

"Off his hand."

"Billy, too?" The lawyer's eyes narrowed.

"Damn' near it. If he pulls through he'll face a murder charge."

The lawyer dropped into the chair behind his desk.

"Police know?"

Johnny shook his head. "I came right here. Thought maybe you'd know some of the answers."

"Maybe I do," agreed Wagman, smoothly. He opened a drawer, reached inside and brought out an automatic. The muzzle was aimed at Johnny's third vest button.

"Up," he snapped. Johnny raised his hands. "Keep 'em up or I'll let you have it." He reached for the phone, keeping his eyes on Johnny.

"Police!" he snarled. The gun waggled. "Sit down. Over there."

"You figure I did it?" Johnny's voice was merely curious.

"What'll a jury think?"

Johnny shrugged.

"And I was trying to get an out for Billy," he complained.

"Oh, yeah? You were trying to pin it on him. Maybe it's been fixed already...."

Johnny said, "No. It was fixed, all right. Too damn' well. Maybe you could explain why you were trailing Eddie and Billy last night?"

The lawyer licked his lips.

"I oughta plug you now. I could say you confessed, then tried to make a getaway...."

"Be your age. That's too raw and too old. Why would I confess and then run?"

The gun lifted a little. Johnny didn't like the light in the brilliant eyes of the man who held it. He decided to talk fast.

"I found something else up there. Maybe you'd like to see it." He lowered one hand.

"Don't try it." The gun menaced and the eyes were dangerous. "If you found anything I need to know about, tell it to me, don't show it."

"A pawn ticket."

"For a ring?" The muzzle of the automatic lowered a fraction.

"Sure," said Johnny, relieved. "At Spigler's." His arms were tired. He rested them on the wall behind his head, felt something smooth and square and cold. The light switch.

"The ticket too, eh? It fits like a glove. You got the ring and the ticket, both. You followed Billy to the boat. You rig up this dumb story but you don't wise the cops. Now you come to me for a payoff, figuring you'll throw a scare into me. You ——— ———"

The phone interrupted his swearing. He reached for it and for just a split-second his eyes wavered, flickered to the receiver.

Johnny galvanized into action. He jabbed at the switch, dived to the floor and crawled to the outer door. It was locked.

There were three sharp stabs of flame and the room echoed with the reverberations. The inside door burst open. A uniformed officer was framed in the light from the waiting room.

"Murder!" screamed Wagman.

The officer drew his gun and charged, tripped over Johnny's outstretched foot and sprawled headlong. His gun roared as he fell.

Johnny made time past the frightened girl at the desk, took the stairs four at a time, got to the street.

HE WALKED PAST the wicket at Spigler's; pushed open the door to the little office at the far end.

The pawnbroker was packing a black bag.

"Get the hell out of here!" he shouted, enraged.

"Take it easy," said Johnny, sitting down. "I've got things to talk about."

"I'll throw you out...."

"Try it," suggested Johnny. "But first, listen. Billy Wilson was sore at you, wasn't he?"

Spigler sat down, suddenly.

"I don't know just why," Johnny continued, "but I suppose you pulled a gyp on him. So he's for getting square."

Spigler looked worried.

"So he gets Eddie Templar to hock his big rock with you. And Eddie redeems it. Swell, so far's you're concerned. Well, Eddie puts the stone in, takes it out. Maybe a dozen times. Naturally, when one day he brings in the familiar setting, you don't stall. You fork over two-three grand. That's the way it went?"

"I don't know what the hell you're raving about," snarled the pawnbroker.

"Um. Well, listen. One day you hear a rumor. Billy's giving the tip he's put one over on you. The stone is in your safe. You look at it. It's paste. And Eddie doesn't come in to redeem it. You're choked and you know it."

The pawnbroker bared his teeth in a sneer.

"Then by and by somebody—maybe Sol Wagman, eh?— comes in looking for flash stuff. A big front but not much dough. You show him this and that. Nothing sells. Then you think of the phoney. You trot it out and Wagman—or whoever it was—likes it fine.

"You give him the lowdown it's phoney but a good fake. He

comes across with five hundred bucks or so and you figure it's that much off your loss. Then Eddie shows up with the ticket."

Spigler cursed in a low monotone.

"Maybe you argue. But Eddie tells you about the law. You know the law well enough. You haven't waited a year; you haven't advertised. And then, Eddie gives you the horse laugh. The stone was insured; you'll have to make good on the policy value. If it was covered for, say, couple of grand more'n it was worth, who could tell, uh?"

Spigler stood up, his eyes pin-points of fire, his hands clenched.

"You're stuck for seven or eight thou. more. You're sore. But you made a bad break, Ben. You warned Billy that you'd get him if he tried to collect. And you damn' near did. But now...."

Spigler smiled. Johnny felt something round and hard in the small of his back, heard a voice say:

"Don't move a muscle except your arms. Stick 'em *high!*"

He raised his tired arms.

"Keep your mitts up." A hand came around from behind him, took the automatic from his shoulder-holster.

"You're going for a little ride, Mister."

Johnny said that was tough.

HE LEANED SIDEWISE, dug back hard with his elbow. There was a cry of pain as he whirled, lashed out with his right, brought a follow-up from his knees. The stocky man who stood behind him simply folded up and slumped to the floor.

Johnny stooped as Spigler came across the table at him. He got the gun, jabbed it hard in Spigler's belly.

"You want it?" he whispered to the pawnbroker. "Just say the word. You'll get it."

The loan shark wilted.

"What you want?" he croaked.

"Turn around. Put your hands behind your back. Stand still." Johnny stooped over the fallen man, lifted him into a chair. As the sturdy body slumped down into the seat, there was a muffled clink of metal.

"Cripes," breathed Johnny. Quickly he patted the pockets of the unconscious man. On the right hip he found the nickeled handcuffs.

"Back up," he ordered Spigler. When the pawnbroker stood close to the table, Johnny snapped one link over his right wrist, clicked the other on the left wrist of the unconscious figure in the chair.

Then he got a flask from his own pocket, tilted back the man's head and poured a good drink down his throat.

The newcomer blinked, mumbled:

"Jeeze, what a sock! *Jeeze!*"

Johnny looked at his knuckles.

"Sorry, sport. But you should have introduced yourself when you horned in. I thought you were one of this lad's mob!" He poked the gun in Spigler's back, none too gently.

"I don't get it." The detective's voice was thick. "They phoned for me to pick up a bird with some stolen property. I thought you was...."

"If I'd known you were a John Law," Johnny apologized, "I wouldn't have scraped my knuckles."

The plain-clothes man started to rise, found himself locked to the pawnbroker.

"Sit down," said Johnny. "Let me do the chinning. This punk is a killer."

Spigler half-turned, spat out, "You ———— liar!"

Johnny grinned. "Nice boy, too," he said. "Spigler is the bird you want for the Templar kill this morning. He trailed Wilson and Templar out to the Stuyvesant Yacht Club, knocked me goofy with an oar, jabbed Billy so full of morphine he won't get over it for a few days and then—cut Eddie into ribbons. Then he tried to frame it so's Billy would take the rap."

"Hell you say!" The Central Office man listened with his mouth open.

"His fingerprints will be on the drawers on the *Jingler*. He was looking for this pawn-ticket, I suppose. I imagine you'll find a hypo of his somewhere; he must have used one on Billy. When Billy gets to talk, he'll give you all the fine points."

"This on the level?" The detective was puzzled.

"Strictly up and up. To make it more so, I'll go to the precinct house with you. And here's your gun."

"We only got the flash on the Templar case coupla hours ago," said the detective. "How'd you get wise?"

"I was on the boat."

"You trailing them?"

"My being on board," admitted Johnny, truthfully enough, "was just an accident. Damn' near fatal, too," he added.

"Who sent in the tip to Center Street, huh?"

"How in hell should I know?" said Johnny, not quite so truthfully.

Pushover

Things got fast and crooked; then along came Johnny Hi Gear

THE BUZZER BESIDE the iron grille purred softly; somewhere in the darkness under the steps of the brownstone front a door opened and closed. A white blur of face peered through the grating at the two Tuxedos waiting silently.

"A private house, gentlemen…" began a husky voice.

The taller of the two puffed his cigarette into a glowing tip; snapped the butt at the door, where if showered sparks on the man inside.

"Open up, fathead."

The door clicked.

"Didn't recognize you, Mister Spillane." The waiter mumbled apologies; used a key on the inner door.

The newcomers brushed past him, walked down a short hall and surveyed the barroom cautiously. A pair of broad, tweed-suited shoulders lounged over a glass of beer; two keen gray eyes watched them in the bar mirror.

" 'Lo, Johnny." Spillane was apparently relieved to find no one else at Feroni's.

The saddle-leather features reflected from the shining glass showed neither surprise nor cordiality.

"George Spillane. Well, well."

The tall man waggled a thin white hand at his smaller, sleeker companion, a gray-haired man whose alert black eyes behind shiny *pince-nez* flashed suspiciously about the speakeasy.

"Know Wagman? Johnny Hi Gear, Sol."

The black eyes made no acknowledgment.

Johnny said: "Had th' pleasure," but his voice belied the words. "What kind of a jam you in, to need a criminal lawyer, George?" he added.

Spillane grinned at the bartender.

"Rye." He looked amiably at the tip of his cigar. "Solly's helpin' me celebrate."

Wagman laughed shortly. "Sure." He ran a manicured fingernail around the inside of his collar. "That's right. Just little whoopee...."

"Celebrating what?"

Spillane lifted his glass with a flourish.

"Hair on your chest," he nodded. "Why, it's like this. Tomorrow night, I'll be manager of the middleweight champ." He drank noisily.

"So?"

"You know it. Mickey'll come through. He'll slap that eight-ball so hard he'll need crutches t' get up."

"Think of that!" Johnny made a design of wet circles on the bar with the bottom of his beer glass. "I thought Tiger Johnson was quite a lad with his dukes...."

"The smart dough says Mickey."

"The only wise money in the fight racket comes in at the box office," said Johnny sourly. "Sometimes it's not so bright then."

"You read th' papers?" Spillane grinned with his mouth, but his brown eyes were humorless. "Them type-jockeys claim it's just a romp for the Mick."

"Um." Johnny slid his glass the length of the mahogany; the bartender caught it deftly and filled it with the same motion. "I knew an expert who guessed wrong on a fight, once."

Sol Wagman bared his teeth unpleasantly.

"Yah! You're one of these in-the-bag babies," he gritted.

"No." Johnny caught the glass as it slid back. "You got me wrong. I didn't say anything was in the bag. What the hell; I wouldn't be holding it if it was."

"I wouldn't." Wagman spat carelessly on the floor beside Johnny's tan oxford. "Somebody might get sore."

Spillane giggled nervously.

"Sol's jumpy," he explained. "He lays two grand on the line that Mickey's winner. You know how it is—"

"I get a bet down, now and then," agreed Johnny easily, "but I don't get rattled about it."

Wagman paused in the act of getting around another rye.

"Nobody can crack wise about this go; it's strictly up an' up. Any muss George has anything t' do with is on th' up an' up."

"Atta pal." George patted the lawyer's shoulder. "No kiddin', big boy, you oughta climb aboard. Guaranteed to fatten the b.r."

"Now I'll tell one." Johnny watched Wagman bite his fingernails and then chew his cigar to shreds. "Good for coughs and colds, makes th' hair grow long an' curly. Spiel me some more."

Spillane chuckled appreciatively.

"You been around, big boy. But, on the level, the Tiger's all washed up. He can box. Okey. Say he can. He can't hurt a Boy Scout with either mitt. There's the payoff; his wallop's gone."

Johnny drank some more beer. The other continued:

"Th' dinge hadda have his own referee t' draw with Tony Casselli. Now, I ask ya. Mickey put th' wop t' sleep ina third. My boy's younger, stronger and nobody ever knocked him off his dogs. He can take it plenty an' give it out th' same way."

Johnny thought fast. What were they trying to build him up for? They knew he was no stray sucker; well, maybe he could find out.

"Who took your dough?"

"Nick-the-Baker," said Wagman, just a shade too quickly.

"You know Nick?" asked George.

"And how. He give regular odds?"

"Don't be a mug like that," complained Spillane. "We hadda give three-two. That's *Telegraph* rating. But Nick's a champhound. Always plays th' favorite. His money's just as good, though."

"Well—" Johnny finished his beer. "Thanks a lot for the inside. I might be interested. See you some more."

"At th' Garden," Spillane called after him.

But Johnny was too preoccupied to answer: his sensitive ear, tuned to Broadway and the roaring fifties, caught a false note in the conversation; his nostrils detected a faint smell of something rotten. He had to find out what was wrong with this picture.

THE FRONT PART of Nikolas Poppolous' establishment just south of the Circle is devoted to confectionery and catering; the rear rooms to somewhat less legitimate enterprises.

Johnny found the fat little Greek engaged in that pastime known as "cutting the book."

"One eighty-eight," wheezed the *patisserie* proprietor. "Odd. Gimme two bucks, Joe."

The slim, effeminately dressed youngster on the other side of the flat-topped desk flipped two bills across the table.

"Goin' t' be busy, boss?" He indicated Johnny.

"That's right, Joe. How you been, Johnny? What's on your mind?"

Johnny waited until the door had closed behind the sleek-haired youth and left only a faint perfume of lilacs behind to remind one of his presence.

"Fine, Nick. You?"

"Things're lousy." He shrugged plump shoulders. "Whatsa use growlin'?"

Johnny lit a cigarette.

"Hear you've picked Tiger Johnson to beat Mickey Brennan."

The Greek studied him from under heavy-lidded sloe eyes.

"That's right," he wheezed. "This Irish is green; he can't box birdseed. Johnson will left hand him to death."

"Brennan can sock," suggested Johnny.

Nick-the-Baker spread his hands in a deprecating gesture.

"Sure. Sure. He can punch. A bag, maybe. Or a setup. He can't kayo what he can't hit. He'll only put a glove on the Tiger once an' that'll be when they shake hands. The nigger's a boxer, what I mean."

"You think Mickey'll lose a decision?"

"Now you said it. The Tiger'll win on points; he'll make that raw kid look foolish."

"Mickey'll have company, then. The newspapers say it's a pushover for Brennan."

"Three will get you two," breathed the Greek, "if you think so."

"I'm just a big-hearted boob, Nick," said Johnny. "But I'll have to dope it out a little longer." The phone jangled; he got on his feet but the Greek waved him back into his chair, picked up the receiver.

"'Lo. Yuh."

"Listen, you big slob." Johnny could just hear the voice over the wire, but it was undeniably the voice of George Spillane.

"No! No!" The Greek wrinkled his forehead and pressed the instrument to his chest as if he wanted to strangle it. "I tell you... I call back.... Not now." He put the phone down and wiped the sweat off his forehead.

"These girls." He looked coyly at Johnny. "Always calling up. A nuisance."

"Must be." The phone rang again, insistently. Nick looked at it as if it were a snake; Johnny said: "Let me fix her." He picked up the receiver before the Greek could stop him.

"'Lo." Johnny tried an imitation of the fat man's wheeze. The Greek grabbed at his arm, made queer little noises in his throat. Johnny stepped back and listened to George.

"Anything goes wrong," said the voice on the other end, "we're li'ble to take a long rap. I do'wanna be mixed up in no—"

"Stop!" screamed the Greek, pulling at the transmitter with both hands and kicking at Johnny's shins. "Stop, I tell you!"

The door opened quietly and Johnny smelled a faint odor of perfume. He put the phone down on the desk.

"This mug causin' trouble, boss?" asked a thin voice.

The Greek panted, looked at Johnny with frightened eyes.

"Mistake, Nick," said Johnny. "That wasn't a girl."

"What did he say?" The Greek held up a warning hand to hold off his patent-leather-haired assistant.

"How in hell could I hear, with you hollering in my ear?"

There was a tense silence, broken by the Greek's asthmatic breathing. Johnny moved towards the door.

"Well, be seeing you," he started; then the pasty face of the boy got in his way.

"Stick around, cluck. Maybe we're not through with you."

Johnny grabbed his mauve necktie, yanked hard. The kid lost his balance, went for his left armpit as he got his chin in the way of a hard right smash. He sagged at the knees; Johnny held him up by the necktie. The color of the boy's face changed from grayish white to dull purple.

"What'll I do with it?" Johnny said to the Greek, quietly.

Nick's pig eyes bulged.

"Outside," he croaked. "In the hall."

"No," Johnny shook his head. "When he comes out of it, I'd get a slug in the guts. No thanks." He dragged the youth to a chair, threw him in it heavily. The shiny hair was all mussed up.

The Greek half rose, in protest....

"Sit down," commanded Johnny. "And don't miss this: framing fights won't send you up river, even if you get caught. But…" he tapped the desk meaningly, "something else might. Know what I mean?"

"No." The Greek became shrill. "You come in here, cut in on my private phone, beat up one of my boys and threaten me… for what?"

"You don't know?" Johnny lifted eyebrows in mock amusement.

"I know this, Mister Gear. If I see you in my place again, I will kill you. You hear me?"

"What you mean," smiled the other, "is that you'd hire someone else to put the mark on me: you're too damn' yellow."

He closed the door softly and went to his garage.

HE HEADED UPTOWN in a hurry, shaving corners, beating red lights and bluffing trucks out of the middle of the street; when he hit the Speedway the dial said fifty-five.

"I don't get it," he murmured to the speedometer. "I don't get it at all. George and Sol build me up to plunge on Mickey but send me to a sharpshooter who says Johnson'll win. Nick is making book for them, of course. The go is fixed for the coon to win; which means that whatever is going on concerns Mickey Brennan. Well…."

He stepped hard on the button.

It was eleven when he braked down at a rambling white farmhouse at Armonk. He parked the car where it wasn't easy to see, strolled up a graveled drive.

The second floor was dark but a light burned in the parlor. He knocked at the door.

"No visitors. Whatcha wan'?" growled a heavy voice.

"This Mickey Brennan's camp?"

"Who wants t'know?" The door opened and a thick-set man with brick-red skin and a badly broken nose stepped forward pugnaciously.

Johnny said, mildly: "George sent me."

The chunky man surveyed him with disfavor.

"Spillane's crazy, sendin' guys out ina middle ofa night. What in cripes' name you want?" He waved a hand towards the lighted room, led the way grudgingly.

"Who's it, Soapy?" A freckle-faced boy of twenty was shuffling a greasy deck of cards. He wore a cook's apron and an old derby.

"I've a message for Mickey," Johnny looked apologetic. "Tough, having to wake him up, this late…."

"That's a mouthful," replied the cook, cheerfully. "Tough for you, if you try it."

"He'll bat your teeth down your throat," rumbled Soapy. "He's grouchy as hell. Never see him so touchy before."

"Leave it till mornin', fella," advised the cook.

"George's orders," lied Johnny. "Private *and* confidential. I can't spill anything, but maybe you birds know…?"

Soapy and the cook exchanged glances.

"Well, now…" The cook was indecisive.

"Jeeze," growled Soapy. "Maybe it's about—" He looked very wise and nodded his head sagely.

"Which is his room?" Johnny asked.

"Upstairs. Second ona right. But don't blame me if you get ya jaw smacked." Soapy Wrinkled his brow thoughtfully, shrugged his massive shoulders.

Johnny went up three at a time.

The door was unlocked. He found a switch, snapped it and sat on the foot of the bed.

Mickey Brennan blinked red-rimmed eyes and cursed thickly.

"Who in hell are you?"

"Name is Gear... Johnny Gear."

"I don't give a damn if it's Clara Bow. Get the hell off my bed." The fighter hoisted a gaudy pair of pajamas to a sitting position.

"How're you feeling, Mickey?"

"You one of them lousy newspaper...?"

"No." Johnny grinned. "But I got a story, at that."

The pajamas came out of bed slowly.

"About a frame-up," continued Johnny, still smiling.

The fighter advanced slowly, menacingly.

"You're one of'm," he snarled, suddenly.

Johnny shook his head, surprised.

"I thought you were regular, Mickey. I figured you on the level. Bet the roll on you. And the tip is out you're going to take a dive." He held up a protesting palm as the other clenched his fists.

"You dirty ———!" snapped Mickey, swinging his right.

Johnny tried to duck, felt surprised at a numbing slap on his face. The fighter had used his open hand.

"Easy, kid." Johnny put a hand to his tingling cheek. "You won't get anywhere doing that."

Mickey swayed on his feet, his left poised for a hook.

"Get out, before I kill you," he whispered.

"Why should you pull a flop, kid? You can beat the Tiger: there's more coin in being champ than...."

This time it was not an open palm but a solid left that caught Johnny on the side of his head: black spots jiggled before his eyes and he felt curiously weak.

He tried to get out a remonstrance, his tongue refused to work. As from a distance he heard the faint words:

"—anything—happens—to—her I'll murder you—"

Then his knees buckled, he pitched on his face.

THE SUN SLANTED early rays into his aching eyes; his mouth was full of gravel and a curious taste. He had the instant suspicion that something more than the blow had kept him so long unconscious. He got to hands and knees, stood up shakily.

He was on the front driveway. He walked over to where he had left his car. It hadn't been disturbed. He got in and drove off.

Johnny stopped at a hot-dog stand for coffee and cigarettes; drove thoughtfully along the Saw Mill River road, tooled the roadster through early-morning traffic downtown to the Metropole.

The first thing he did was to look in the telephone book, but he did not use the phone. He grinned cheerfully and turned on the shower.

Half an hour later, his favorite waitress in the Coffee Shop inquired solicitously about his scratched face.

"Accident," he explained. "I ran into a man."

"You have to be careful driving, the way people are," she sympathized.

He finished his scrambled eggs and read the sporting page of his newspaper. The columnists thought it was a walkover for Brennan, unless— Bill Kessler said Mickey would put the

Tiger away in the early rounds, barring— Henderson spoke of the passing of a champion, but played safe with a postscript about a lucky punch or a reversal of form.

Johnny decided against the roadster, flagged a yellow and gave an address in the nineties. The driver thought his fare looked all in, figured he was going to hit the hay after an all-night bender. So it was a surprise when Johnny tore a five-dollar bill in half, gave him one section.

"Stick around," he said. "I'll be needing you. The other half, when we're through."

"I'm with you," the driver said fervently. "Anything short of crime."

"It might come to that," grinned Johnny and went into the Sylvara Arms.

HE EXAMINED THE bell-board, pushed one marked 4C and walked up three flights. At the door of 4C were two quarts of milk. He rang.

"Good morning, Mrs. Brennan," he said to the blonde young woman who opened the door.

"What is it?" She looked scared, her voice trembled.

"About Mickey," he explained. "May I come in?"

She stood aside without a word.

He walked into a neat and rather expensively furnished living-room.

"Mickey's worried," he began abruptly.

"Oh!" She did not seem surprised. "What—?"

"I thought maybe you could help. He's likely to lose his fight tonight. You wouldn't want him to do that?"

"Oh, no, no. But what can I do? What can anybody do?"

She put her head on the arm of her easychair, started to cry softly.

"Well, if *you* don't know—" He looked about the room. Maxfield Parrish lithographs, red damask draperies, blue Chinese rug, a piano with some music open on the rack, some books on the table, a child's toys.

A child's toys. Johnny commenced to see light.

"Go away," she sobbed. "Please go away. You can't do anything."

He got up, patted her shoulder.

"I might be able to," he said and went out, closing the door softly.

Downstairs, he got to the street, went through the delivery entrance and found a gray-mustached man in overalls sweeping the area.

"Where's Brennig live?" Johnny's voice was bored. "Got a bicycle for Brennig."

"Brennig?" The man leaned heavily on his broom, puzzled. "Guess you mean Brennan, huh? No, there ain't no one there rides a bike. Unless maybe it's training apparatus. That's Mickey Brennan, the fighter."

"It's a kid's bike," continued Johnny, showing no interest.

"That's funny. The Brennan kid is only three. Don't seem like she'd ride a bike, now, does it?"

"No. Must be wrong party. Obliged, anyway." Johnny went away.

He found the taxi-driver in a doze. "We're going places," he informed that individual. "We're going to try and pick up a girl."

"Jake with me, boss," chuckled the driver, smiling broadly. "I can show you a few ———...."

"Be your age," snapped Johnny. "This is a three-year-old. She drinks lots of milk and likes picture books."

"Oh!" The driver seemed disappointed. "Where'll we look?"

"How about a pastry shop? Youngsters like sweet things." And Johnny gave Nick's address.

The *patisserie* was crowded; clerks handled eclairs, cream-puffs and fancy cookies—a pleasant smell of frosting and ice-cream was in the air. Johnny got to the rear door unnoticed, walked into the Greek's private room without knocking.

He looked over the office carefully before going in. Nick sat alone at the big desk.

He smiled unpleasantly.

"So," he murmured. "You dare to come?'

"Cut the bull," said Johnny, curtly. He disliked theatricalism outside the theatre. "Where's your pet snake?"

"Joe?" The confectioner lifted eyebrows, astonished. "But Joe has gone to the bank for me."

"Oh, yeah? Think it's safe to trust a heel like that in a bank?"

The Greek spread expressive hands.

"You didn't come to be funny…?"

"I'll say I didn't. Sit down and stay set." The other subsided like a punctured tire. "I came to ask if you know the rap for kidnaping in this state?"

The fat man smiled derision.

"And if I did, what's it to you?"

"It's life," continued Johnny. "A long rap. You've ten, maybe twenty years to run, if you keep clear of the law and watch your heart."

The Greek adjusted his necktie with a grimace.

"You like to hear yourself talk?"

Johnny stared at him.

"If the Brennan girl isn't home by six o'clock, it'll be just too bad for you, Nick." He watched the other's hands, moved where he could see the door better.

Nick got up from the desk, kept his hands in sight and walked around to Johnny; then he swung the door open with a flourish and bowed low.

"I'm not buying any birdseed today," he sneered.

Johnny turned to face him, lifted his left arm just enough to make it easy to get at his shoulder-holster.

"Don't move a muscle, mister," said a thin voice from the desk. "And don't go for that rod unless you're tired of livin'."

Johnny cursed himself for being taken in by the old gag; a man under a flat-top desk.

He waited, listening. He heard nothing but a swift intake of breath; then he saw a great flash of white light, felt a crushing pain at the back of his head and slipped slowly to the carpet.

THE FLOOR UNDER his feet felt damp and clammy; he put out a hand... it was cement. Then that was why he couldn't see; he had been thrown in a cellar. His head swam with dizziness and his stomach rebelled with periodic nausea, but he was still alive. He wondered why.

Nick wasn't the sort to stop at a little thing like murder. That repellant creature of his, Joe, was a killer if he'd ever met one. Yet he was alive—he felt his legs and arms, got shakily to his feet—when he should have been dead.

He listened. Above, he heard faint sounds of feet; the customers in Nick's glass-and-gilt shop. There was no light at all in the cellar; he felt for matches, found that they had been taken, along with his gun, his knife and his watch. But his money was intact.

"Crying out loud," he muttered. "Why would they—?"

He tilted his head painfully, strained his ears. Surely that was something moving, over at the right.

He dropped on all fours; crawled forward with a hand in front of his face. A faint rustling came out of the blackness; then ceased quickly.

Johnny wiped the sweat out of his eyes and stretched out a hand; recoiled.

He had touched warm flesh. Still, there was no sound; the expected attack did not materialize.

Again he ventured an explorative hand; then laughed grimly and got to his feet. He bent down and picked up a limp and almost inert body; a child.

He fumbled for her hands; swore viciously when he found them wet and sticky from blood where the rope had chafed. He got the bonds from her ankles, put his fingers on her face. She was gagged and blindfolded. He held her tenderly.

"It's all right, now," he whispered. "Everything's all right now."

The girl moaned faintly, found she could use her tongue and began to scream hysterically. She kicked and clawed feebly.

Johnny put her down.

"Easy, honey," he said, gently. "Don't hurt yourself. I'm friends. Everything's all right. I'm going to take you home."

She moaned something about "—bad man's—tell mamma—" and subsided to a steady whimper, punctuated by an occasional sob.

He held her by the hand and commenced an examination

of the cellar. It was clear to him now: they were going to pin the kidnaping on *him*. He had walked right into it with his chin out.

He would be found hiding, with the girl; Nick and Joe would swear that he had brought her into the store. Mrs. Brennan would tell, innocently enough, of his visit; the police would interpret it as a veiled attempt at extorting ransom. Probably George Spillane would get into the picture in some way; Mickey would tell his tale—Johnny groaned.

"What a mess! Well, something's got to be done and done fast."

The child had, in all probability, been blindfolded all the time; so far as she knew, Johnny was the "bad mans" who had taken her away from home. He frowned in the darkness; perhaps not even the fact that he was—unofficially—an under-cover man for the commissioner's office would clear him of a charge like this. No, decidedly, he had to get out of it. Besides, he remembered with a rush, there was the fight tonight, and Mickey would be taking a beating, unless—

That was how they worked it, then; Mickey had been warned that if he won the scrap he'd never see his daughter again. So, with everything to gain, from beating the Tiger, he wouldn't dare to win.

Johnny's fingers identified barrels of supplies which his sense of smell proclaimed glucose, sugar and gelatine. Cases of eggs, milk-cans full of syrup and boxes of fruit-flavor were piled along the walls. But there were no windows and only one door. That was at the top of a short flight of wooden steps; the door was of heavy steel, fireproof. It fitted so tightly that he could not see even a glimmer of light from the other side; his efforts made no impression on it whatever.

The little girl had stopped crying now; he continued to talk soothingly about home and mamma and supper and she followed him blindly as he attempted to explain that he was trying to find a way out of the giant's castle.

He made the rounds of the damp cellar once more, with no expectation of success. The sounds of tramping feet overhead had ceased; his wrist-watch had stopped but he figured it was closing time—probably nine-thirty or so. Wearily he leaned against the wall and held the child in his arms; she went to sleep instantly, her head on his bruised shoulder, one hand clutching his lapel.

"In the morning," said a voice beside his ear. "That's time enough."

Johnny was so startled he nearly dropped the child; it was Sol Wagman's voice. But as he stood away from the wall, it vanished. He leaned back again, pressed his ear to a cold metal surface.

"Tip off the dicks that this punk was seen with the baby yesterday, huh?" Nick was speaking.

Johnny set the girl down, shook her awake. She held fast to his knees.

He got his ear to the sheet of metal again, but the voices had gone. His fingers investigated; he whistled softly.

"Dumb-waiter," he murmured. "Now maybe...."

The door to the shaft was nailed in; he tried to force it loose with his fingers but only broke his nails in the attempt. Then he sat down on the floor and thought for a long minute.

He got up, kicked an iron hoop off a glucose barrel and went back to the shaft door. By leaning his weight on it, he managed to push it in far enough so that the heads of the nails projected sufficiently to let the steel hoop get underneath. A hard yank and a nail was out. The rest was easy.

He pried open the door and looked up; faint light filtered down from the floors above. He got the rope, pulled hard. The car and rope were locked in position.

He said a few reassuring words to the child, who began to cry again; climbed into the shaft and went up the rope, hand over hand.

Ten feet up he got his feet on a sill beneath which came light and a warm smell of cooking; he took a moment's breather and shoved hard on the door.

HE HAD NO time to notice that he had emerged into the hot and smelly bake-shop or to decide what to do next. Five feet away, stupefied by his sudden appearance, stood Joe.

Johnny made a flying tackle from the level of the dumb-waiter just as the gunman started shooting. One bullet twitched at his shoulder, the next buried itself deep in the floor.

They sprawled in a heap; another shot ploughed into the plaster above as they wrestled for the gun. Johnny got a clamp on Joe's wrist, twisted until the bones cracked. There was a muffled explosion and the killer coughed weakly, collapsed.

Another shot came from the doorway beyond. Still crouching over Joe's body, Johnny wrenched the gun from the fingers of the dying man, took careful aim and fired.

Nick-the-Baker looked very much surprised, took a step backwards and fell against the door-jamb, sliding slowly to the floor.

"Only one more bullet left in this thing," shouted Johnny, "but if you think I can't plant you with it... come ahead." He got to the door, grabbed for Nick's gun with his left hand and shoved his right hand into the hall.

At the other end, a door closed softly. Johnny sprinted down the hall, jerked open the door. He saw a leg going around the corner of the big door into the main room of the pastry-shop, fired a snap shot and chuckled when he heard distant curses before the door was bolted.

He used the phone in Nick's office.

"Bellevue? Talking from the caterer's store at Fifty-seventh and Broadway. Yeah. There's a couple guys here been playing around with firearms.... Yeah. They got hurt all right—better call headquarters. Sorry I can't wait."

He hung up, unlocked the cellar door and switched on the lights. The girl was still crying; still very frightened. He picked her up, got the delivery door open and started to carry her down the street.

A cab pulled up beside him.

"You found her, huh, boss?"

Johnny breathed relief.

"Lord," he sighed. "I'd forgotten about you. You've earned your dough." He climbed painfully into the cab. "What time is it?"

"Quarter to ten, buddy. You look as if you had been in a war."

"I have. Say, be a good scout and do some shopping for me, hey?"

So Ann Brennan got cookies and milk, which was the best Johnny could think of; he explained later that he was unused to feeding girls under twenty.

Also, she had a face-wash and a comb with Johnny's own comb; then she went soundly to sleep while the taxi-driver risked all their necks by looking back over his shoulder while he dodged Eighth Avenue traffic to the Garden entrance.

Nobody pays much attention to what anybody else wears at the Garden fights; dress-suits can rub elbows with mechanics' overalls and no one notice. But the sight of a man dressed in a blood-soaked tweed suit, a torn collar and a very soiled shirt, carrying a three-year-old girl to the ringside, caused a certain amount of neck-craning.

Some of the press-boys thought it would do for a human-interest item and wondered what it was all about, during the interval while Iron-throat Joe was announcing the final go.

Ann woke up because of the glare of lights and the noise of the crowd. But she did not recognize her father. He was dressed in a bathrobe, for one thing; and she was too tired and excited, for another.

Johnny tried hard to get Mickey's eye, but he couldn't get a flicker. The challenger sat with his eyes fixed on the canvas in front of his chair; he mitted the crowd without looking up.

Then Johnny was in a sweat of apprehension lest the fight be thrown in the first round. Mickey came out listlessly, let the Tiger do the leading and took every opportunity to go into a clinch. His footwork was dead and his punches had no snap or sting.

The crowd booed, the sports writers cast knowing looks at each other and the broadcast announcer told his radio audience that this was, apparently, just another one of those things.

The second and third rounds were even worse. Tiger Johnson kept his left in Mickey's face like a burr; he swayed and slipped the few pepless punches which the Irishman threw his way with ease and grace and he gained confidence and speed as all worry of the outcome left him.

"He's going to take his dose in the next round," said Johnny to the girl. "We'll have to do something about it." She looked up with round eyes. "That's your papa in the ring there. Your papa is fighting for you. You say 'hello' to him."

"Hello, papa!" she piped. Her voice was drowned in the crowd.

"Oh, louder than that," he said. "Scream as loud as you can."

The gong rang for the fourth. The negro rushed across the ring and put a left to Mickey's nose.

There was a chorus of "Ahs!" from the crowd, then silence.

"Now," said Johnny, lifting her high above the seats. *"Shout!"*

"Papa," she shrieked. *"Papa!"*

Mickey took a left hook flush on the mouth to listen; then he backed around to see where that voice came from. Ann waved a hand at him and screamed again. The negro landed a hard right to the belly.

"He's going," yelled the knockout-hungry crowd. "There he goes—"

But Mickey wasn't going anywhere. He just wanted to make sure his eyes weren't fooling him. Johnny waved at him, grinned broadly.

"Go get 'im, Mickey," he hollered. "We're *for* you."

"BRENNAN LOST THE first four by a wide margin," called the radio announcer above the roar of the crowd. "But at the finish of this last session he got home his first real punches of the fight. He hit the champion with a straight left that staggered him and followed it up with a right hand smash to the heart just as the gong rang. Here goes the bell for the fifth."

Mickey came out like a flash; swinging and ducking. The

Tiger was overconfident now; forgot to cover up. Brennan put a left to the face, another to the chin. The Tiger went to the ropes, bounced back and lashed out with a short right.

Mickey took it flat footed; swung from his ribs with a grunt. The sound of the blow went clear up to the top girders of the Garden.

Again the Tiger back-pedaled. But now Mickey was savagely aggressive. He showered rights and lefts to face and body, took a hard sock to the nose that started claret flowing.

"*Wow!*" yelled the crowd.

They stood toe to toe for a second; the Tiger gasping for breath because of body punishment; the white boy with bared teeth and a wrinkle of concentration on his forehead.

Suddenly there was a smacking sound, like two hands clapped together hard. The negro started to reach out for Mickey's arms—that last attempt to stall and clinch which is the sure sign of a losing fight—

Mickey stood away, measured and landed a left from his knees. Tiger Johnson swayed stupidly, fell on his face in the resin.

Brennan tried to wallop the referee when he came to raise his hand in token of a new champion; called dazedly for "George" and mumbled something about "baby—home."

Johnny had to fight his way to the ringside; halfway there someone came shoving through the crowd, unceremoniously jostling the fans right and left.

" 'Ray for the Champ," someone started the shout. " 'Ray for the Champ," others took up the chorus.

The champ took Ann from Johnny's arms and started to cry.

"Where's George?" he mumbled. "George oughta—"

"George has probably taken the first train West," replied Johnny as they made their way to the dressing-room. "If he knows what's good for him, he has."

"My wife—" said Mickey, thickly.

"I phoned her. She knows about Ann. Everything's all fixed up, Champ. You can take the kid home."

Mickey sat down on a chair and pushed his rubber away.

"Lemme be," he muttered. "You say George was—mixed up in this?"

Johnny nodded.

"Along with a couple of other birds. They're dead or damn' near it. Nick-the-Baker and his trigger-boy, Joe."

Mickey stroked Ann's hair.

"And Wagman?" He searched Johnny's face for an explanation of the kidnaping. "Was he—?"

"He rigged it up," answered Johnny. "He was too smart to do any of the dirty work. But he planned it. I'm pretty sure."

"I'll break every bone in his—" growled Mickey.

"You better wait," suggested Johnny Hi Gear, "until his leg heals up. He's got lead poisoning in his right leg."

600 to 1

*Johnny Hi Gear, under-cover man, takes
a shot on a policy king at long odds*

THE BROAD-SHOULDERED MAN in shirt-sleeves filled his pipe slowly without removing his eyes from the tobacco.

"Forget it, Joe. You don't have to song and dance about it. Consider the four bits a tip and call it square."

The bell-boy wrinkled the black skin of his forehead into a protesting frown.

"I ain't givin' you no song an' dance, Mistah Geah. You win three hundred berries less my ten cut... but it's like I'm tellin' you. I can't pay off until Doogey shows up... an' nobody's seen him since las' night."

Johnny Hi Gear walked over to the window and looked down.

"Okey, Joe. Send it to me for Christmas."

Tears welled up in the black boy's eyes.

"I ain't handin' you no line, Mistah Geah. If I had the dough, I'd pay off myself... but Lawd, I ain't no bankah."

Johnny turned, wearily.

"What the hell, kid. If you lost it at craps—you lost it. It doesn't keep me awake nights. I've never let a welcher worry me."

Joe gulped back the lump in his throat, fumbled in his uniform and produced a cheap and battered wallet. From it he took a five and three ones and laid them on the dresser. Then he walked to the door:

"Nobody's got a right to call me a welcher, Mistah Geah. I

give you the straight of it… an' I'll pay back ev'y lousy dime outta my own pocket."

He opened the door.

"I'm a son-of-a-gun," said Johnny, "if I don't think you're on the level. Give me the low-down… who's this Doogey person?"

"My cousin," answered Joe. "He's a no 'count niggah but he'd nevah take no runout powdah on me… I'd bust his brains out. That's what's funny." He got out the wallet again and handed Johnny a printed business card.

Johnny read it.

J. DUMONT WILKERS

Investments

4114 Fifth Avenue

New York City

"Very tony," he said. "Does he run this policy himself?"

"I don' think so. He's got about a dozen runnahs… like me… workin' on commish… but I think he turns it in. We had plenty winnahs befo'… he nevah turned us down on biggah wins than this one."

"You have any other customers pick a hot one yesterday?"

"No sah. Only you, Mistah Geah. Sometimes I go two, three weeks without no ten per cent cut."

Johnny slipped on a lightweight coat and a Panama.

"I'll take a look-see. Where's he live?"

Joe showed white teeth.

"That's his house," he indicated the card, "—he ain't got no office except his straw. But he ain't home. I went there this mawnin'."

"Sunk without a trace, eh?"

"How's that?"

"Never mind. He wasn't in?"

"No sah. His wife was in… she tol' me he went out 'bout ten o'clock. She figured he was cockeyed an' I guess he been ginnin' up some anyhow."

"Yeah? Why did she think he was drunk?"

"Las' thing he said was somethin' 'bout goin' out t' look at some fiddles and a bowl."

"That's cuckoo enough, all right. And he didn't come back?"

"No sah."

"What time did he usually have his payoff money ready?"

"Around ten sometime. You think they's somethin' fishy?"

Johnny nodded.

"Begins to smell slightly putrid," he agreed. "He never hinted to you who his boss was?"

"Nevah heard him talk about no big shots, no sah. What you aim t' do, Mistah Geah?"

Johnny shoved him to the door and walked with him to the elevator.

"Cousin Doogey needs attention," he said. "What kind of attention depends on where and how… I locate him. Don't collect any more policy dimes until I see you, Joe."

He took the "Down" car, walked to the subway and got a Lenox Avenue local.

HE GOT OFF at 135th Street, walked east and entered a dilapidated brownstone that had once been the pride of the élite north of the Park.

Three flights up he located a door on which was nailed an aluminum strip bearing the punched letters *Wilkers.*

He tried the knob gently and then knocked several times. He put an ear to the panel; the apartment within was very quiet. But a thin thread of light at the sill showed lights were burning inside.

He took out an old envelope, scrawled the words "About Doogey" on it in pencil and slid it half underneath the door; then he walked heavily away and clumped down the stairs.

When he tip-toed back a minute later, the envelope was gone. Johnny grinned cheerfully.

"Round one to the challenger," he said to himself. "Now, to get inside." And then he noticed that the door was slightly open.

"Now that's too good to be true," he murmured.

He kept close to the wall and pushed the door wide open with one hand; the other was not far from his shoulder-holster.

The hall was half-lit from the illumination in the front room.

"Hello," he said, loudly. His voice echoed dully.

He went in, cautiously; the living-room… an ornate affair of blue plush and shiny oak… was quite empty. An early morning tabloid was open on the table and the room smelled of stale smoke.

The kitchen was next and that was empty too.

In the bedroom he found clothing scattered on the floor; toilet articles overturned on the bureau and a chair tipped on its side. The bed had been slept in. An end of a pink silk nightgown had been caught in the closet door and protruded a few inches, as if the door had been hurriedly closed.

He pulled it open, standing to one side.

The body of a young negro woman toppled out of the musty, clothing-filled darkness; he caught it before it fell and put it on the bed.

She had been choked to death. The torn state of the nightgown, the scratches on her cheeks and the contorted condition of the death-set features showed that she had put up a struggle.

Johnny surveyed the corpse morosely.

"I hadn't expected to find you," he muttered. "I'm beginning to take a real dislike for this husband of yours."

He wiped his fingerprints off the closet door knob and considered. The woman had evidently been dead some hours;

the body was quite cold. But there had been someone in the apartment when he knocked at the door and tried the knob; someone who had taken his scrawled message and then opened the door to make his entrance easy.

That person had not made exit by the front door... Johnny hadn't had it out of his sight when he walked down the hall. Then, there must be another way out. The fire-escape, of course.

He went back to the kitchen. The window was closed, but unlocked. It opened on the fire-escape. He got the window open, looked out.

A figure came running down the alley; halted under the fire-escape... then another. Familiar figures, these were, in a familiar uniform.

"Bulls," growled Johnny.

Whoever had been in that apartment some minutes before, had made a getaway and phoned the police... with the intention of trapping Johnny. That was why the door had been left open....

He was caught, right enough. Those steps on the stairs... those would be more policemen. They would leave one man in the hall for a guard, the rest would make a search... and he would be caught with the body of a murdered negress.

What good would it do to explain that he had a number in the secret files of the under-cover division? One of the rules of the game was to disown such men, when they were caught in a jam. His position was that of a spy, caught in the enemy's country, in wartime.

He stepped to the outer door and bolted it; that would give him a few extra minutes, perhaps.

"Open up," yelled a bass voice. "Open that door."

Johnny said nothing but did plenty of thinking.

"Break it down," said the bass, lower. "He'll never get by Finnegan and Swartzy... smash it in."

A bulky shoulder caromed against the thin door panel. It cracked and the whole door groaned.

Johnny got out his gun and put a slug through the top of the panel, maybe seven feet from the floor.

"The next one'll be lower," he growled.

He heard a whispered consultation outside; then he ran to the kitchen window, stuck his head out and hollered in as deep a bass as he could command:

"Hey, Finnegan!... Swartzy! Okey. We got him! Come on around!"

The figures in the alley below held a brief consultation.

There was a gruff:

"Comin' up, Sarge." They vanished around the corner of the house.

Johnny went up the escape at a rush, sprinted across the roof to the fire-wall on the adjoining building and vaulted it when he saw them come back on the run, their guns drawn.

He found the trap-door to an adjoining roof, walked casually downstairs and joined the crowd that was beginning to gather.

THE DISTRICT SWARMED with men in blue and men in plain-clothes. The ambulance, arriving to receive the body of the dead woman, had attracted a crowd as honey draws flies.

The medical examiner had reached the scene and Central Office men had taken over. Patrolmen from the 135th Street station guarded the exits from all nearby apartment houses on the block and another cordon covered the street. The roofs were being searched by Homicide Squad hard-boileds.

Johnny finished a cigarette and thought things over. He had some dope which those headquarters men could probably use; on the other hand, the matter had taken on a distinctly personal aspect.

That he had been cheated out of a policy prize was a small enough matter; that someone had attempted to pin a murder on him was otherwise.

Then again, if he talked to the police, there was just a chance he would get Joe the bell-hop in bad trouble. Joe had admitted seeing Mrs. Wilkers that morning… it might occur to thick-headed cops that he had seen her even later. Also, Joe had a possible motive against the Wilkers family, even though it concerned Doogey and not his wife.

He approached the belligerent officer who stood at the steps of 4114.

"Anybody by the name of Wilkers hurt?" he asked innocently.

The cop glared.

"What business is it of yours," he growled. "Keep movin'."

"Because," continued Johnny, calmly, "I might give the police some information."

"Hey, Ike," bellowed the bluecoat. "Here's a guy stickin' his nose inta trouble. Talk to him, will ya?"

Another uniform appeared from the dimly lit hallway; a sergeant by his stripes and badge.

"What's *your* name?" rumbled a deep bass.

"Gear," said Johnny mildly. "I come up to see a party by the name of Wilkers. Can I go in?"

"You cannot." The sergeant advanced, got an arm on Johnny's. "What'd you wanna see him about?"

"He owes me some money."

"Oh, yeah?" The sergeant wrinkled his brow in perplexity. Then deciding the matter was one concerning which he should protect himself by passing the buck; "You'll come with me, mister."

"Am I under arrest, officer?" Johnny had difficulty in repressing a smile.

"You save your yap," said the sergeant, "for the Inspector."

Upstairs, he was led into the plush and oak living-room, where a tired-faced man with iron-gray hair surveyed him with annoyance.

"Well, well. What's your story?" asked the Inspector.

"Mister Wilkers owes me some money. I came to collect and found a lot of cops...."

"Um. When'd you last see him?"

"I never saw him."

"How'd he come to owe you money, then?" The Inspector became heavily sarcastic. "Borrow it over the phone, or something?"

"No," said Johnny. "I won a policy prize yesterday; he runs the pool. My runner couldn't get uptown to collect, so I came myself."

"What was your runner's name?"

Johnny looked blank.

"Joe something or other. He's elevator boy or bell-boy in my hotel... why, what's the trouble?"

"I'll ask the questions, "snapped the inspector. A burly plain-clothes man came into the room from the hall. "What's that you've got, Steve?"

The detective opened his hand and Johnny didn't even have to crane his neck to see the little enameled lapel button. It was very fussy with blue and red and gold, but the picture was simple enough.

"Three violins?" The Inspector was puzzled.

"Sure. One of—" began the Irishman.

"Oh!" The puzzled look on the inspector's weary features disappeared. "Well, that doesn't mean a thing, now. Go right after it, Steve. I don't give a damn about policy pickings, but *murder*. That's different!"

Steve went away and took the button with him. Johnny had a feeling he had stumbled into a live lead, so he became as matter-of-fact as possible. The inspector took his name and address, smiled sourly when Johnny gave his occupation as "speculator" and advised him to be ready to appear for further questioning, or as a witness, should he be required.

"A woman has been murdered," he finished. "You will find it best to say nothing about this to anyone."

"Oh, I won't," said Johnny, his face a picture of surprise. "Not a word." The sergeant ushered him downstairs.

HE THOUGHT IT out over coffee and a western in an all-night wagon on Lenox Avenue.

"The button," he said to his cigarette, "was a means of identi-fication… well known to the police. That's probably the hookup between Doogey and his boss. And this morning, several hours before she was strangled, Doogey's wife said he intended to go out looking for fiddles and a bowl… well, the three violins are fiddles, all right. Bowl, fiddles… everything but the pipe.

> He called for his pipe, he called for his bowl,
> And he called for his fiddlers three.

Then he used a phone book, but found no Cole or Coal listed in Harlem.

It might be a nickname; he might be all wet about it, anyway. But he tried another angle. He spoke to the short order cook.

"I borrowed a fiver from a sport by the name of King Cole, coupla months ago," he said confidentially, "and I'd kind of like to pay it back. I've had a little luck with the doggies and I'm flush… but I forgot where this bird hangs out."

The big-lipped counter-man took the bait:

"You musta forgit his name, too, big boy. O'ny high-steppah ah knows by that handle's King Collis."

"Lord. That's right, 's name was Collis."

"Bad guy t' fool with, boss."

"Is that right?"

"You spoke a piece. You owes him sugah, you-all bettah pay up, else yo find yo-se'f daid some mawnin'."

"I'll remember that," said Johnny.

He got the Collis address from the directory, walked the long block to Seventh Avenue and north. The house was one of the newer apartments in Harlem's swankiest section; the doorman and elevator boy looked like Balkan generals.

"The King in?" he inquired of the latter.

"Mistah Collis? I'll see, sah. What name, sah?"

"Wilkers."

The boy sat at the switchboard and plugged in.

"Mist' Wilkers t' see Mist' Collis," he said. And, after a second's pause: "Yessah… that's what he said, sah… Wilkers." He listened for a moment, unconcerned. Then he laid down the receiver.

"Third flo'… Three B." He led the way to the elevator.

Johnny pushed the gilt button beside the mottled green and old-gold door of 3B with his left hand; but the precaution was not necessary, for the individual who opened it looked harmless enough.

He was about forty and dressed as if he were seventeen; the mauve shirt and lilac four-in-hand harmonized beautifully with the tan suit and shoes. He might have passed for white anywhere save in the South; his eyes were not the shining brown or glistening black of the full-blood: they were deep, dull gray, oddly lusterless… fish eyes in a slightly swarthy face.

The dead, listless eyes surveyed him disinterestedly.

"What," his voice was unpleasantly shrill, "is the idea?"

"I wanted to see you," said Johnny.

"Well, take a good look."

"And talk to you," added his visitor.

"Go ahead, spiel…."

"About Doogey."

The narrow eyes squinted slightly, the dapper man stood aside and waved a negligent hand.

"Come inside," he invited. "What about this fellow?"

"He's disappeared. And his wife has been killed. The cops are after him."

The other shrugged.

"He does some work for me," the shrill voice was unimpressed. "What did you want to see me about?"

"You've no idea where he might have gone?"

"Jeeze, what a question… he might have gone a million places and I'd know nothing about it. Why ask me?"

"Well. He was one of your collectors…."

"And if he was?"

"Then maybe you paid him off last night?"

"Sure. Sure, I did. What's it to you?"

"I picked the right numbers, but I never got my three hundred dollars… that's what it is to me."

"Oh. Well, don't get sore at me. Take it out on him, when you find him. There's little enough in this lottery when you're giving 600 to 1, without making good on runners that skip out. Sorry." The dull eyes said that the interview was over.

"You wouldn't know how to reach him?"

The other stopped with his hand on the door knob.

"Listen, Mister Whatever-the-hell your-right-name is. Get me right. I don't know where Doogey Wilkers has gone and I don't give a good damn. He's been drunk half the time and he's been scrapping with his wife. I suppose he knocked her off and jumped a freight. Now, are there any more questions you'd like to ask?"

"One," said Johnny. "How did that envelope get on your carpet?" He pointed to an old envelope, with the words "About Doogey" scrawled on the back; it was lying under the table in the lobby of the apartment.

King Collis stared at him.

THE NEGRO TOOK two paces towards him, bent forward a little at the waist and made a lightning-like grab for the back of his own collar.

Johnny cried out sharply:

"Don't. You go for your knife and I'll blow your belly to hell and gone… take your hand away from that chiv… *now!*"

Collis put his hand at his side and straightened up but his eyes never changed expression.

"Sit down in that chair," said Johnny, "and sit damned still if you want to eat again. Now, you merry old soul, tell me just what you were doing over at Wilker's house a couple of hours ago."

Collis kept his mouth closed.

Johnny kicked him in the shins, hard.

"Ah!" The impassive features writhed. "All right. I was there. But I didn't bump the woman... honest to God."

"I wouldn't believe you if you were telling the truth," said Johnny. "Go ahead, spit it out. Why were you there?"

"Doogey asked me to come. He said I could help straighten out some trouble between him and his skirt... but when I got there, Doogey was missing and his wife was dead."

"So you waited until I showed up, and then sicced the cops on me, hey? Birdseed!"

"It wasn't me that rang up the bulls. It must have been Doogey...."

"You think 'em up faster than I can turn 'em down," complained Johnny. "But talk your way out of this one. Doogey had a date with you last night... probably a settle-up. His wife hadn't seen him since that time, when she was asked about it, this morning. You were the last one seen with him; you were the last one known to be with his wife before the police arrived."

Collis licked his lips.

"Except yourself," he shrilled. "You're a hot one to be tagging me for this business; you can't put it over, either. If that bum had a date with anybody last night, it was with some sweet mama of his own; he's probably beat it with her while you're bagging away...."

Johnny shook his head in admiration.

"You should have been an auctioneer, King Collis. You can sell damn' near anything. But not that line of bull. The voice that tipped the station was high and shrill… and if that isn't your squeaker, I'm Primo Carnera."

"Anyone can imitate a voice."

Johnny thought of the deep bass, grinned and said:

"Even up. You sure shoot a swift line, sport clothes. But where were you, last night, after ten?"

"Right here. Ask the doorman. I was with two of my—uh—assistants."

"Well. It wouldn't be hard to get a couple of your runners to swear to any smooth alibi you can cook up, that's a fact. But your flossy chatter hasn't got you clear yet, King Cole. Let's have a peek at the domicile."

Johnny kept his gun in his hand while he forced Collis ahead of him through the six rooms of the big apartment. There was no sign of any other than the owner's occupancy, until they came to the kitchen.

"What's going on here," exclaimed Johnny. "An Old Home Week or a Foundryman's Picnic, eh?"

The kitchen table was piled with platters of meat, dishes of butter, bottles of milk, other bottles of whiskey and ginger ale, cold potatoes, tomatoes and several kinds of fruit.

"Just cleaning up," said Collis. "Help yourself, you want anything."

"Thanks so much," said Johnny. "I'd be afraid of powdered glass or arsenic. Why don't you put 'em away… they'll spoil, this hot weather."

The dapper policy king seemed hardly to notice what he was saying.

"Go ahead, stick 'em in the Frigidaire… even if you get collared, you may get bail and then you'd use this junk."

Collis made no move.

"What the hell. It's cheap. Let it go," he said, edging away from the kitchen.

Johnny frowned.

Then he got it.

"Collis," he said, softly. "Open up that ice-box."

The mauve collar of the harmonious shirt was damp with sweat. Collis opened his mouth as if to speak, but desisted at the sight of the muzzle of Johnny's automatic.

He walked across the room, mincingly, and threw the latch to the huge ice-chest, swung open the door.

"Holy Cripes," breathed Johnny.

The refrigerator was full of flesh and blood; human flesh and human blood. From the top shelf, there leered at him the horrible face of a young negro… the severed head stood upright on the shelf.

The torso was shoved in the large center space and the legs and arms had been hacked in two to enable them to be crowded in.

Johnny gagged a little and turned to the policy operator.

"Shut it up," he gritted. "And if I don't shut you up for the rest of your natural, may I be a ———— ———— Sit down on that floor. No, get up… walk ahead of me, to the phone. Don't give me a chance to plug you, because I'd love to do it…."

Johnny remembers walking as far as the lobby entrance… after that his memory is limited to a crashing, numbing smash beside the ear and a flash of blinding light that blotted out everything.

HE WOKE UP to hear himself say "Ah-r-r-r"… there was a splitting pain in his head and vicious stabs along his legs. It was several seconds before he realized that he was being held up by a pair of enormous hairy black arms, his mouth was stuffed with a bad-tasting cloth and someone was kicking savagely at his shins, sending waves of nauseating pain all over his body.

"Teach you, you ———! You'll crack my shins, will you?" He heard the shrill, taunting voice and then passed out again.

The next thing he heard was:

"You'll kill him, suah, boss…" in a different, deeper tone. He was lying on the floor, now, and the frenzied Collis was booting his ribs and arms heavily, until his body was one flaming ache….

"That's what I mean to do to the ———" squeaked the high voice of the policy operator. "But I'll make him suffer first." He drove a brutal toe against the tender side of Johnny's head, where the life-preserver had struck, Johnny almost fainted once more.

There was a moment of silence; Collis sank back in a chair, exhausted by his rage and his exertions. Johnny opened his eyes.

Standing above him was a tower of a man; a great hulking figure with ape-like arms and a ridiculously tiny, bullet-shaped head. Johnny saw the huge hands and thought of the prodigious thump which had knocked him out; of the bluish-black marks on Mrs. Wilkers' neck….

"You're a bright lad," wheezed Collis. "But not bright enough to outsmart the old King. That letter dodge was bean-work," he went on as if talking to himself. "It never occurred to me that you might have prepared a duplicate envelope and dropped it on the floor. I found the other one in my coat pocket just now. I wouldn't have admitted anything about being over at Wilkers' flat if you hadn't pulled that fast one—and you wouldn't be getting ready for the big jump, right now… like that Wilkers' woman who knew too much and was ready to spill it."

Johnny felt too sick and sore to say anything, even if the filthy gag had not been crammed in his mouth.

"But you were dumb, not to think that someone else might have a key to my place. The Singer here is just a midget," he laughed hysterically, "but he'll do in a pinch. Hey, Singer?"

The giant negro chuckled.

"Lucky Ah came in jes' th' right time," he said.

"But there's one thing I can't get," continued Collis. "Midget, take that rag out of his kisser… I wanta ask him something… and if he makes a squawk louder than a whisper, you sock him."

The Singer came over and fumbled with a string that held the gag in place; tore it away. Johnny felt as if he could spit cotton; his jaws were numb and his tongue was as thick as a beefsteak.

The policy King walked over and stood above him.

"Who tipped you off that Doogey had talked to his wife about meeting me?"

Johnny did a Paddock with his brain.

"The bulls," he managed, with an effort.

Collis face twitched as if he had received an electric shock.

"Give it to me right, you ——— or I'll cut out your heart and fry it. When did any bulls talk to you about me, hey? I've got the flatties in my district walking a chalkline when they meet up with one of my buttons—I think you're a lousy liar."

Johnny croaked:

"That was it. They found one of those identification buttons that you gave your collectors—and three fiddles—over at Doogey's. The inspector said to bear down on you; that any arrangement they might have had went overboard in a case of murder."

"He said *what?*" The dapper man's voice was a screech.

"He said to get you and to hell with any grafting setup; that murder couldn't be bought off in his territory." Johnny watched the effect of his words on the two men; the Singer was obviously scared stiff while King Collis was frantic with rage.

"Why, the double-crossing ———! I had those buttons made to keep my boys out of trouble with those blues. I've got enough on him and his captains to send 'em up for fifty years. They said to *get* me?"

"Sure. They've got some kid who talked to Mrs. Wilkers this morning… he told them about your seeing Doogey last night. They've got your button and some of your fingerprints. And," Johnny made a wild stab, "they've got something on you about some other runners of yours who disappeared the same way.…" He appeared not to notice the look of fear which came into the dull eyes. "They figured that whenever you ran short of dough, you knocked off whichever runner had turned in the big winners the previous day… then you got credit for the payoff and kept the money too. The cops said that 600 to 1 wasn't long enough odds for you… you had to wipe out the one."

Collis stored at him, through him, impersonally. His hand went slowly up to the back of his collar, came out with a thin, keen blade of steel.

"Boss," said the Singer.

"I'll shut your trap for keeps," said the policy king to Johnny.

"Somebody at de door, boss," repeated the Singer.

Collis turned, scowling ferociously at the interruption.

The door bell was ringing, insistently.

THE KNIFE HESITATED a foot from Johnny's stomach… he watched it, fascinated and powerless to avoid it.

The racketeer straightened up and a worried look came into the ordinarily lifeless eyes.

"Watch that door, Singer. No one comes up unannounced unless they're looking for trouble. We'll give it to them."

The Singer got down on hands and knees near the door. There came a series of heavy knocks, the sort a nightstick makes on a metal door… then the Singer crawled back.

"Sounds like po-leece, boss," he muttered. "Ah don' crave no ruckus with po-leece."

"Shut up," snarled Collis. "Go get that shotgun and some loads."

The huge man started away reluctantly.

"Boss," he protested. "Ah don' mind fightin'… you knows that… but these blues 're likely t' turn a typewriter on… Lawd, I hates machine-guns."

The thumping on the door sounded again.

Collis went into the bedroom and started packing papers in a suitcase; the giant returned to the living-room with an ugly-looking snub-nosed shotgun. He was shaking with fear.

"Singer," whispered Johnny without moving his lips, "listen to me. Go out in the ice-chest… bring me a shot of booze, will you? There's an open bottle of gin there.…"

The negro looked at him stupidly.

"Go ahead," whispered Johnny. "Take a shot yourself… you might need it. Hurry up, before he gets back."

The Singer began to grin, slyly.

"Ah gits yo'," he husked and left the room.

Ten second later there was a howl of gargantuan proportions; a thundering roar of fright and uncontrollable terror; Johnny watched the bedroom door.

The Singer came lumbering through the hall in a panic of fear:

"Yah... h... h... h! Wha... a... a...!" he howled.

Collis stood at the door, with an automatic.

"Stop it!" he said in a flat, emotionless voice.

"Kee... ee... ee," hollered the Singer. "His haid... his haid jumped at me.... Oh, Laws...."

"Cut it! *I said cut it! Singer!*" The flat voice intoned.

The big negro got to the front door, turned the knob.

"*Crack,*" said Collis' gun.

The Singer stopped, still blubbering.

The policy king walked towards him leisurely.

"You don't cross me up, easy as that," he said softly.

The Singer held his belly with both hands and coughed once or twice; then he dropped like a shovelful of dirt.

Johnny thought it queer that the cops should waste all this time getting in; the knocking had ceased. His chance try to get the weak-minded Singer to open the refrigerator had worked; but it had only left him worse off than before. There was no hope of splitting the opposing forces now, for one of them was already half dead.

Collis came over to him, holding the still-smoking automatic.

Johnny smiled weakly and said:

"Doogey, his wife, the Singer. A nice score you chalked up, King Cole."

"Don't forget yourself," said the even tone. "You'll make an even number. How would you like it…?" He took out the blade, held it in his left hand, the gun in his right. "You pays your money… you takes your choice."

Johnny clenched his teeth.

"You owe me three hundred dollars already," he stalled.

"You'd never spend it," said Collis. He lifted the gun, got it around to Johnny's chest. "This way is quicker."

Johnny shut his eyes; never expected to open them again.

He wondered whether a man killed by a gunshot hears the sound, listened carefully and heard a new voice say:

"Hold th' pose… just like that."

Johnny got his eyes open in time to see Collis whirl and snapshoot at a blue uniform; heard two almost simultaneous reports.

Collis hunched his shoulders, looked down at his gun in surprise.

He started to say something, his knees buckled and he crashed to the floor, half on Johnny.

The cop and another man with him helped Johnny to his feet. The patrolman looked at the blood and bruises on Johnny's cheek.

"What in hell's been goin' on?" he asked.

"Collis," Johnny wiped some blood out of his eyes, and indicated the dead man, "had an ice-chest full of dead nigger; I happened to find it out so he tried to finish me, too. The big fellow by the door was his right hand. He got scared and tried a runout; Collis shot him."

"This the policy big shot?" asked the officer.

"Sure," said the other man. "Sure. I been super here two years now; he's been here all the time. I only knocked on his door to tell him he threw a lot of good fruit away in his garbage this morning; then I heard some shooting, so I call's you…" he turned to the bluecoat.

"A break," said the policeman. "Saved this bird's life sure." He looked at Johnny, curiously. "He beat you up some?"

"Plenty," agreed Johnny. "He's the killer that strangled the Wilkers woman, and…" he bent over the body and dug out a fat wallet, "he owes me three hundred bucks. I'm collectin' right now."

"Here," began the cop. "I don't know about that…."

"Jeeze," said Johnny. "You'll get a promotion and a raise in pay on my say-so… I'm entitled to what's mine."

"Well…" The cop went to the phone, asked for the precinct.

"That a *Journal* you've got?" Johnny asked the janitor.

"Sure." The janitor kept his eyes away from the blood and the bodies, shivered a little. He handed the newspaper over and watched while Johnny looked at the seventh race summary at Aqueduct.

"Playin' the gee-gees? You sure don't seem to let a beating up bother you…." The janitor was openly admiring.

"No," said Johnny. "Policy. They use seventh race now, instead of clearing house totals. I like to keep an eye on the numbers, that's all."

"I never fool with that stuff," said the janitor. "Odds are too long."

Johnny smiled grimly.

"I've taken longer chances than 600 to 1."

Table Stakes

*Johnny Hi Gear plays for the stakes on the table
and finds they are only part of the game*

THE SALLOW-FACED MAN passed a manicured hand over his bald and perspiring dome and shifted uneasily in his leather chair.

"Come on," he exclaimed irritably—"bet or get off...."

The big man in the white linen suit looked up.

"You seem to be in a hell of a hurry to lose more dough, Lou," he said mildly. "I'll bump it again."

Louis Santolo grunted and met the raise. None of the others at the table spoke as the next cards were dealt—a queen of clubs to Santolo and a trey of hearts to the broad-shouldered man.

"That don't make it any worse," said the bald-headed player. "Let's make it interesting." He shoved two bills into the center of the green felt; the light from the drop-shade showed the figures 1000-1000 clearly.

"Here they come, down our block," said the man across the table. "Two and two is four, they tell me." He slid a packet of fifties and hundreds into the pot.

Santolo chewed on the stump of a cigar, frowned and raised again; this time five of the bills with the four-figure mark.

"What a man," grinned the other. "Eats raw meat for breakfast. Well, I can stand it if you can, Lou." More piles of smaller bills joined the yellows in the center of the table.

The breathing of the three players who had dropped out of the hand became noticeable; somewhere on the Post Road, a car backfired and Santolo twitched nervously.

"Sevens beat treys, the way I learned it," he said through the cigar-butt. "Maybe you got tens with 'em?"

"Maybe I have." The man in the linen suit didn't smile. "But it takes dough to find out."

Santolo swore and saw the raise.

"Show 'em," he grunted.

The big man turned over his hole card.

"Three little threes," he said, reaching out a hand towards the money with a questioning look. "Good?"

Santolo shoved back his chair and stood up; then he flipped over his down card; a queen of diamonds.

"I got enough," he snarled. "That's the lousy luck I been runnin' all night; threes over two pair; straights over threes… that washes me up."

One of the men who had been watching the play rose and put on his coat.

"It's three anyway," he said. "How much you win, Johnny?"

The man in linen stacked the bills into a neat pile.

"A grub-stake for Saratogo," he answered.

"Must be close to fifty grand," said another of the group. "Table stakes is your game, big boy."

Santolo stood with his back to the table, staring out a window at the dark waters of the Sound.

Johnny got up and found his hat.

"Give you a chance for a come-back whenever you say, Lou." He stood beside the squat figure of the bald-headed man.

"Jake with me, Johnny," said Santolo. "I can afford it; you ain't heard me bellyachin', have you?"

Johnny Hi Gear shook his head slowly.

"You're a good loser, Lou," he answered. He tucked the bulging wallet into his inside vest pocket, held out his hand.

Santolo put a moist and flabby palm in it, smiled thinly.

"I'll get hunk one of these days," he said.

"Any time you say," said Johnny.

HE TURNED THE key and opened the door of his room at the Metropole, clicked the switch. There was no answering blaze of light and he started a quick backward step when a pleasant voice said:

"Come right along, Mister Gear. Don't raise your mitts or your voice. Just step right in."

Johnny's eyes searched the blackness of the room beyond; the lighted hall made it impossible to see the speaker who was evidently in the darkest corner. He failed, too, to recognize the voice, but saw the wisdom of the advice.

"This light suit would make a swell target," he said stepping inside.

"Close the door like a nice boy."

Johnny did as he was told; as he turned a circle of white light hit his bronzed features.

"At this distance," the intruder's voice was cheerful, "It could put a slug through that pearl stud of yours… so don't start anything."

"I didn't think Lou would try anything as crude as a stick-up," said Johnny.

"Lou?" The man in the dark was surprised. "Lou who?"

"Don't make me laugh," said Johnny. "You want my roll?"

"Mind reader," said the other sarcastically. "Chuck it on the floor in front of you… and don't make a pass at that shoulder-holster or I'll drill you."

Johnny tossed the fat wallet on the floor.

"Go and sit down on the bed," said the unseen visitor. "And be nice and quiet or you'll go to sleep damn' sudden."

Johnny sat as near the foot of the bed as he dared, put out his hands on either side as if he were tired. His left hand got a good grip on the blanket which the chambermaid always kept neatly folded at the foot of his bed.

"How much you got in here?"

"You ought to know," said Johnny. "Didn't he tell you?"

There was a crackle of crisp paper and a noncommittal grunt from the dark corner, but Johnny's eyes were now accustomed to the dim illumination reflected from walls and ceiling by the beam of the flashlight. He could make out vague outlines of a burly figure in the armchair beside the desk; saw something which he figured was a gun in the right hand.

For just a split second the white beam wobbled as the man with the gun tried to handle bills and flashlight with the left hand… and Johnny swung the blanket up and out; flung it as a bullfighter casts his cape. He followed the thick folds of the woolly cloth; leaped sidewise to avoid a shot which never came and saw the flashlight's beam smothered for a moment.

The intruder had half risen from the armchair and Johnny hit him with a hard shoulder which sent them both sprawling on the floor. Johnny caught a knee in the groin and said "Ah—h—h" very painfully; then he clamped a forearm where the throat should have been and got a stabbing elbow in the belly for his trouble.

He tried again, took a glancing fist on the temple and saw dizzily dancing lights for an instant… found a thick windpipe and put everything he had left into a bulldog grip.

The man beneath him, half-smothered in the blanket and slowly choking, put frenzied strength into savage kicks with his heavy boots… the blinding shock of the pain nearly made Johnny let go, but he squeezed a little harder, felt the body under him go limp.

He held on for a moment, fearing a trick, but the man had collapsed.

Johnny found the flashlight, got the gun and pulled off the blanket.

The man on the floor was blue in the face with congested blood; his lips were clayish and his bulging eyes were sightless. He was a huskily built individual of perhaps fifty, well dressed and well groomed.

Johnny threw a glass of ice-water from the tap into the purplish face, ripped collar and necktie from the thick neck.

His uninvited guest gulped, coughed, gagged and finally caught his breath with an agonized spasm of strained choking. Johnny propped him against the wall and brought more water. The other looked surprised and put shaking fingers to his bruised throat, wagged his head from side to side slowly and waved the water away.

"Now," Johnny sat wearily in the armchair, "tell me why I shouldn't call the bulls."

THE MAN AGAINST the wall looked at the bills scattered on the carpet and massaged his windpipe gently.

"Any reason why I shouldn't turn you in?" Johnny picked up the phone.

The other groaned.

"Do me a favor—phone the police."

Johnny put down the instrument.

"What's the story?"

"No story. Call the cops, Mister Gear."

Johnny frowned.

"No rush about it," he said. "What a crust you've got, trying to put the bite on me like that."

The man on the floor touched a swollen cheek tenderly.

"You're pretty handy with your dukes, fella," he moaned. "Oughta be able to knock a lot of big ones into the little ones with 'em."

"Is that a crack?" Johnny came over and stood beside the chunky man. "If it is, say it plainer—and funnier."

"Atlanta's no joke, Mister Gear—"

"Well, well," Johnny saw light. "So you're a detective—is that the line?"

"Federal operative 645," said the other. "Warrant's in my pocket—search and seizure, John Doe."

Johnny followed his eyes to the scattered money.

"The dough?" he inquired.

The detective smiled patiently. Johnny jabbed the captured gun into the man's chest hard.

"Listen, Sherlock," he said softly. "I'm no bricklayer, but what I get I get on the up and up. No strong-arm stuff; no up-the-sleeve racket. Just plain risking my roll against the other guy's. So," he poked the gun harder, "open up that ugly yap and tell me why you jack me up in my own room at five in the morning."

The plain-clothes man leaned over and picked up one of the yellows.

"Not bad," he said admiringly. "Not bad a-*tall.*"

Johnny went back to the chair thoughtfully.

"Phonies?" he asked, and knew the answer before he got it.

The government man looked bored.

"Well, now—seein's you don't know anything about it—the paper came from Dalton okey, but these photo-engraved duplicates are always a little coarse. The ink's McCoy—and the impression's good enough, only it wasn't done on C Street."

Johnny lit a cigarette, his mind racing at top speed.

"You figure I been shoving that junk around?"

The operative shut his eyes and opened them slowly.

"Lou tipped you off then."

The other shrugged.

"Some guy that was sore as hell phoned in the dope—I don't know who this Lou mug is. Your partner?"

Johnny smiled grimly.

"I might make you a proposition," he said.

The detective grinned broadly.

"That's more natural. Course, I couldn't take a bribe, but I like to hear 'em offered. Always makes me feel righteous or something. Once in a while Washington'll exchange clemency for an extra good set of plates—but that's another matter. What's your figure?"

"My ———" said Johnny. "You're a dumb bunny. Can't you get it through that fat head of yours that these were planted"— He indicated the scattered bills—"Worked off on me? I'd as soon give you a sock on the nose as a bribe. But I'll still make you the proposition."

"Well?"

"You want an arrest, maybe a conviction. The government wants the plates this queer was made from. I want about fifty thousand bucks of real money."

"You and me, too."

"Shut up. If I get a break, I might fix up all three at one pass."

The government man leaned his head wearily against the wall and sighed.

"Save it for the front lawn, mister," he said. "You got me right and I'm makin' no yelp—but spare me the baloney, please."

Johnny pulled on his coat and found his hat.

"Stick by the phone—right here," he said at the door. "If I phone you by seven you can bring along some bracelets—"

The federal agent narrowed his eyes.

"And if you don't?"

Johnny smiled frostily.

"Then I'll tell you where to send the ambulance," he said.

JOHNNY USED A phone book, grabbed a Checker and gave a West Seventy-fifth Street address. He watched through the rear window of the cab for a minute, to make sure he wasn't being tailed; then he tried to figure out how Santolo had been able to get in touch with a federal agent so swiftly and how the latter had acted so speedily on his information. He decided that the tipoff had been planned well in advance of the stud game the previous night.

In that case, the Italian would be expecting some sort of reaction from Johnny's supposed arrest; he might even anticipate being investigated himself.

"Maybe I better not disappoint him," Johnny murmured to the taxi-meter. "Drop me at the corner of Columbus Avenue," he added to the driver.

In a lunchroom he found a phone booth.

"Good morning, Lou," he said presently.

"For cripes' sake! What's the idea draggin' me outta bed at this hour'n the morning?"

"I'm in a bad way, Lou...."

"Yeah? And where do I come into your jams?"

"It's about those grand bills you lost... they're duds."

"What in hell you talking about?"

"On the level. I've got a treasury man beside me now; I told him you might know where they came from, Lou."

"You must be nuts... I don't know a ——— damn' thing about any of your lousy money. Don't try to drag me into any mixer either... you'll wish you hadn't."

"You wouldn't give me the cross-up, would you, Lou?"

Santolo cursed loudly.

"Now, I'm wishing you, Johnny—don't horn me in on your

sob-story: I don't know anything about any money and—"

"The dick is coming up to talk to you, Lou."

"Hell he is—" the receiver clicked.

Johnny got a cup of coffee and a roll before he strolled over to the Midlorn Arms, a tony ten-story structure with a gilt marquee and a decorative fountain. A milkman was carrying a wire tray full of white bottles across the sidewalk.

"Hi!" Johnny hailed him. "Two extra creams for Santolo—throwing a party tonight."

The milkman grinned appreciatively.

"Kayo… Santolo… that's 7D, ain't it?"

"You said it," Johnny answered. "Thanks a lot."

He took the automatic elevator to the seventh and pushed a pearl button in a marble slab.

"Who is it?" The voice inside was wide awake.

"Mr. Santolo?" Johnny altered the pitch and timbre of his voice as well as he could. "I'm looking for Mr. Santolo."

The door opened a fraction of an inch and Johnny put his shoulder to it. The door banked back suddenly.

"You—!" said the man in pajamas. "You lousy ————!"

"Don't be tough, Lou," said Johnny. "You're in wrong as it is. You can't bull your way out with that line of horse. Go into the living-room—or wherever you keep your checkbook."

The Italian kept his eyes on the gun in Johnny's hand and backed from the hall into an ornately furnished Spanish room.

"Where do you keep your checks—?" Johnny began, as the bald-headed man turned towards an elaborately carved desk. *Stand still*—against that wall. I'll get the book; tell me where you hide it?"

Santolo snarled:

"Use your eyes, you ———!"

Johnny found the black-covered book; studied the stubs for a second.

"Now I've got forty-two pieces of paper," he got out his wallet, watching the other carefully. "Which I'll exchange for just one. These thousand-buck bills *might* be good; someone told me different. I see you've close to thirty-thou left in the bank."

The Italian opened and closed his hands rapidly.

Johnny tossed a fountain pen and the check book on the big side table.

"Sit down and write," he said softly. "Make it out to yourself, sign it and endorse it. Not that I don't trust you, Lou—but the banks don't like to stop payment on that sort of check."

The Italian went a pasty white under his swarthy complexion.

"You'll never get away with it," he said shrilly.

"Maybe. Your stubs might be all wet and the check might bounce back, of course. But, Lou," he leaned over the other's shoulder, "I'll never be found with counterfeit dough in my pocket... and that's something."

Santolo ripped the check from the book with an oath and held it out; it dropped from his trembling fingers and fluttered to the floor beside a bronze-green pedestal lamp with an ornamental Venus in marble holding a conch-shell lamp. The Italian muttered something thickly and lunged after it; his shoulder crashed against the white stone figure—sent it toppling to the floor.

Johnny dived at the falling statue before he thought; reached out and caught it as the Italian, on his knees, said sharply:

"Drop it—drop the rod, or I'll shove this through your belly."

Johnny caught a glimpse of a knife blade, cursed himself for allowing his eyes to stray from his man, even for a second.

He let the gun fall to the carpet.

"My error, Lou," he said.

"MUSCLING IN LIKE some ——— damn' flatty—I'll say you made a slip, big boy." The Italian recovered the gun and slid the knife back in its sheath under his collar.

"My Fed friend'll drop in any time, Lou. You don't want to make any breaks."

Santolo laughed unpleasantly.

"What you think he'll find?"

"Maybe some engraved plates."

Lou said: "Now I'll tell one. He'll find a dead sucker."

Johnny shook his head and kept his eyes on the other.

"Twenty's about the limit for forging and uttering—but they give you the chair for murder in this state," he said.

"No murder," grinned Santolo. "Maybe suicide—or accident. But not murder—"

"I might get you off the sentence if you're willing to turn up the plates that Washington boy wants—that would be safer, Lou."

"If this treasury baby can find any plates on me, he's good. No Civil Service cop has anything on little Louis. But you— you're too mouthy to live. I'll send a wreath of poison ivy to the funeral."

Johnny said nothing, but his lips tightened a little; this cold-blooded counterfeiter was in deadly earnest—that was sure.

"The kitchen," said Santolo. "Go ahead of me into the kitchen."

Johnny walked down the hall and entered a tiny room with a set tub, an electric refrigerator, a gas stove and a kitchen table with two gaudily painted chairs.

"Sit down and make yourself comfortable—for a minute." Santolo chuckled at his jest.

Johnny used one of the chairs, saw the Italian, with the gun held ready, drag out a gallon jug from under the set tub.

"Make my own gin sometimes," explained the bald-headed man. "This is first-class alky here."

"I'm not thirsty," said Johnny, getting an inkling of what was coming. "Be sensible, Lou—you don't want to be running away from a first-degree rap all the rest of your life."

"Don't worry about me—you'll wish you could run in a few minutes."

The Italian went behind the chair in which Johnny sat; there was a gurgle and Johnny felt a cold liquid soaking his neck and his back—an overpowering smell of alcohol nearly stifled him and he shivered as the fluid evaporated and left him chilled.

"Cool?" taunted Santolo. "You'll be warmer right away."

The icy liquid splashed over his face and stung his eyes with a searing fire; he sensed it as the first of those unbearable pains which would follow the match which Santolo would light when the alcohol was soaking every inch of his clothing and skin. He might as well die with a bullet in his body as be burned to a crisp that way—and through the pain in his eyeballs and the fear that made the hackles rise on the back of his neck, he suddenly realized that it took two hands to hold a gallon jug while it was being poured!

With the first flash of the thought, he turned and leaped; heard—rather than saw—the jug crash to the floor; got his arms around a chunky body, banged it against the stove with every ounce his pain-tortured body could muster.

The suddenness of the attack had surprised Santolo out of using the gun; now there were two dull, muffled shots. Johnny heard them as from a distance, being engaged in getting a fold of skin at his throat away from the teeth of the enraged Italian—but he realized that he must get that gun in a hurry.

He hooked a right to the sharp chin of the other; smashed a left to the same spot and felt the gun with his right hand. He slowly twisted it; blood trickling from his throat and tears streaming down his face from the blazing pain in his eyes—twisted until the muzzle pointed in—

"Now... you ———!" he gritted, "pull that trigger again, will you?"

The Italian glared at him savagely; gouged at his eyes with the clawing fingers of his free hand. Johnny threw his weight forward, bent the shorter body of the other back and back—

"Santa Maria!" gasped Santolo. "Let me—breathe—"

"Where are those plates?" growled Johnny pushing harder.

But the man had fainted. When Johnny released his grip the chunky body slumped to the floor like a sack full of beans.

Johnny stuck his head under the cold water faucet. Then he wiped his eyes and put a cold, wet handkerchief on the raw wound at his throat. He looked at the figure under the stove.

The sallow skin was leaden; splotched with brown flecks of dried blood—and when he felt for the heart he could not detect the slightest beat.

"I hope I haven't killed you," he said soberly. "That would be letting you off easy."

HE STRIPPED OFF his soaking clothes, got under the shower and let the cold water run for a long time. Then he found a sky-blue satin dressing-gown and put it on; in the pocket was a dry pack of cigarettes.

His eyes were red-rimmed and stinging; his throat ached and burned alternately and there was a peculiar feeling at the pit of his stomach. Fortunately, Santolo's first two shots had gone wild; he had not been hit at all by the Italian's bullets.

He went into the living-room.

By the big writing table he looked on the floor for the thirty thousand dollar check and his wallet full of dummy bills. There was nothing on the floor.

His eyes went to the door; it had been closed. He went over and tried the knob—it was locked.

Someone had come in the apartment while Santolo had had him in the kitchen—someone who now had close to a hundred thousand dollars' worth of good and bad money plus a negotiable check.

Was that person still there? Johnny put his hand in the right-hand pocket of the dressing-gown, where he had put the gun, and went through every room. In the bedroom he found pink and silky garments scattered everywhere and a long-handled hairbrush beside the powder puff on the bureau. In the kitchen Santolo sprawled ridiculously in torn pajamas in a wet smear of blood and alcohol. Johnny knelt and listened; there was no pulse that he could detect, but the faint sound of breathing was unmistakable. The Italian was alive.

If there had been a girl—and the evidence was clear—she would probably have a key to Santolo's apartment; the unknown visitor might have been the owner of the lingerie in the bedroom. But if that had been the case, why did she come and go without making her presence known? If she had come when Santolo had the upper hand there was nothing to fear. If, on the other hand, she had arrived during the fight—she might have been expected to call for help.

Johnny found a half-full quart and poured a stiff drink. He sat in one of the kitchen chairs and watched the ashen color in the Italian's face turn lead-blue, then purple and finally pasty-pink.

Johnny poured himself another shot of rye and considered the matter; everything about the affair had been unnatural. Lou had lost important money with too easy a grace to be natural; the Federal man had watched him depart to look for Santolo with too little concern to be natural, and now there was this disappearance of the check and the queer money—

"Dio Mio!" groaned the man on the floor.

Johnny nudged him with his foot.

"Come out of it, you dirty little wop," he said.

"Ah!" Santolo opened his eyes. "My back—it's broken."

"No such luck," said Johnny. "I just cracked the yellow streak in it. Tell me who was the girl who beat it when I came in?"

The other looked blank.

Johnny took the gun out of his pocket and used the barrel on the Italian's shins.

"Yah ———!" Santolo squealed with pain. "I'll talk."

Johnny leaned back in his chair.

"You better," he grunted.

"What you want to know?" The man on the floor grimaced with agony as he half-raised himself on one elbow.

"Don't stall. Who was the wren?"

"Stella."

"She beat it—with your dough and mine."

Santolo tried a grin; showed uneven teeth.

"Where are those plates?"

"I swear to—"

The revolver barrel swung out and down.

"Jeeze—don't hit me—she's got 'em. Stella."

Johnny stood up.

"And where is Stella now do you suppose?"

The other rubbed his sore shins, but made no reply.

"You're too crooked to trust anybody that far, Lou. You'd never let a girl get anything like those plates on you. That's one for the book—now tell me where they are."

A fat bead of sweat dribbled from Santolo's chin, but he shivered as Johnny bent over him.

"Don't—please don't!"—the girl's voice caused Johnny to whirl and almost to press the trigger—but she was unarmed and disarming enough with her worried, fearful frown and the confusion of blonde hair under the tiny blue cloche.

"Don't hurt him any more—I'll show you the plates," she said tearfully. And from the doorway she beckoned Johnny into the living-room.

JOHNNY LOOKED HER over; a trim number, he decided—and too innocent looking not to be dangerous.

"I've never shot a woman," he said, "but this gun has four good bullets left and—" he motioned her to come in the kitchen. "Where's your bag?" he added.

She seemed surprised at the question, glanced quickly at Santolo—who was making frantic signals to her from his position on the floor.

"Get this straight, Stella," Johnny got between the door and the girl, "what I want is my dough, not Lou's kickoff. If he hadn't tried to pull a firebug act on me I wouldn't even have given him those belts in the shin—but your boy friend's just plain nasty. Now, Lou gave me some dud bills over the stud table and I made him give me a check for what he had left in the bank in exchange—I lose ten grand at that. Then you come along and pinch the check."

She said: "No," very emphatically.

"Give me that check—and I'm off selling my papers," he continued. "Those plates—I needed them for a lever, that's all. And unless Lou turns them in—he's due for a bad jolt when the treasury boys catch up with him. But that's his hard luck— what I want is that check."

"I haven't seen it," she said. "My bag is in the living-room— but there's nothing in it, you want."

"Let's see," he said. "Lou, get on your feet—stand up and don't make one wrong move, or—"

Santolo groaned.

"I can't," he wailed. "My back's hurt—hurt bad."

Johnny yanked him to his feet with a jerk.

"It's up to you, Lou," he said.

Santolo tried to look puzzled.

"Stella's probably fixed it so that check will be cashed as soon as the bank is open," Johnny explained. "You have just two minutes to make her tell her story—then I'll go to work on you again."

The Italian grimaced.

"You win," he whispered. "Turn it over, Stel'."

Stella shook her head, slowly.

"I told you," she drawled, "I didn't get any check."

Santolo burst into a stream of filthy invectives, made a step towards the girl with his hands clawing at her face. She screamed and stumbled over a chair, fell to her knees, shrieking.

"Don't let him—get me—honest to ———— I didn't keep it—"

Johnny got a grip on the neckband of the Italian's coat where the knife sheath was sewed, wrenched the other erect.

"Be good," he snapped. "You're just the baby that would try rough-housing a woman. *Lay off*—hear me?"

Santolo subsided, cursing steadily.

"She's a—liar," he mouthed. "She's got 'em all, the dough, the check and the plates—the dirty little double-crosser."

Johnny laughed.

"I guess I'll have to let you handle her, in your own way," he said. "But not until I'm gone—I don't like to see even a gunman's sweetie beaten up, while I'm around. And since you can't make her talk without killing her, I'll have a try at it."

Stella got up.

"Thanks, mister," she said, breathing heavily, so that the thin wax-like nostrils dilated like those of a frightened animal. "You're not a bad gee; I can tell you enough about this bum to send him away for life—" She indicated the Italian, contemptuously.

"Sweet of you," murmured Johnny. "But I'm not interested. What I want is my money."

"I haven't got it," she said. "This louse was expecting you and told me what to do—but you gummed the works by starting that riot before I could horn in—"

"You were to cut in on the party? Was that it?"

She nodded, pushed the little hat back on her forehead, wearily.

Santolo snarled and turned towards Johnny.

"She's a ———!"

Johnny slapped him in the mouth.

"I don't want to hear what she is," he growled. "Not from you, wop." He looked from the Italian's contorted features to the still-frightened face of the girl. "But I think you've been played for a sap, at that. Something tells me little Stella hasn't been on the square with her sugar daddy. Am I right, Stella?"

She extracted a powder-puff and a mirror from her stocking, powdered her nose before replying.

"I hate his guts," she said, deliberately. "He's a cheap little four-flusher and he beat me up every time he got cockeyed."

Santolo seemed to shrink in height; he tensed his muscles and crouched imperceptibly; his clawing fingers worked convulsively.

"Behave," Johnny warned him. "Or I'll let you have it."

Little pin-points of golden light burned in the great, dark eyes of the Italian; the full, red lips drew back slowly over the irregular white teeth.

Johnny shifted his aim so that the gun pointed at the right shoulder of this wild-eyed Italian who seemed oblivious of all except the figure of the blonde girl. He didn't want to kill the other, unless it became necessary.

And then he became aware of something round and cold which pressed insistently at the back of his neck.

"DON'T LET ME intrude," said a voice which Johnny had heard once before that night.

Johnny lowered the gun; saw Santolo's eyes leave the girl and travel to the doorway behind his back.

"How'd you trail me, Washington?" He didn't turn his head to ask the question, because he was watching the girl. She was smiling, now—and her eyes said that she knew this man for a friend.

"Lou been actin' up, Stella?" The treasury man pushed Johnny suddenly, so that the latter nearly crashed into Santolo.

She tucked a blonde curl under the tight brim of the cloche.

"He's a rat," she said. "You got here just in time, George."

Johnny had turned and faced the government man.

"I thought you were working from the inside," he said. "But I'll admit I didn't know you were playing ball with Lou, here."

"How'd you guess?"

"You didn't take time enough to examine those thousands… if they were as good as you said, you'd have needed a glass. So, it was a cinch you knew all about them. Then, Lou didn't seem much surprised when I phoned him you were coming up to see him."

"Bright lad." George was sarcastic. He stepped inside the kitchen door. "Any other things you doped out?"

Johnny looked thoughtful.

"Well, it took no heavy brain-work to spot Stella for playing around. I suppose you got the check?"

George smiled unpleasantly.

"*And* a lot of evidence," he said, smoothly. "There was some honest-to-goodness money in that billfold of yours, too."

Stella spoke, nervously:

"Why all the finagling around, honey—let's get going."

George didn't look at her.

"One more thing, baby—and we'll breeze. I want those plates."

Johnny looked at Santolo; the Italian was white with rage and his eyes were luminous with murderous desire.

"C'mon, Lou—spit 'em out," said George. "You want to get your teeth knocked down your throat?" His voice rose, as he asked the question and he advanced, menacingly.

Santolo controlled his features with an effort, shrugged expressively.

"And if I do?" he whispered.

George laughed, harshly.

"Kayo, with me," he said. "Stel' and me will make tracks for British Honduras—where there ain't no extradition laws and a man can get genuine booze. Hurry it up, Lou—that's all I want."

Johnny saw the glint in the cold, blue eyes of the man from Washington; thought it unlikely that anyone except George and Stella would leave the apartment alive, once the plates were handed over.

"I get the dirty end of the deal," Santolo said in a low voice. "I fixed this whole setup for you, George—and you fall for that little ————!" His voice trembled, as he looked at Stella.

"You shut your dirty mouth," she shrilled, "or George'll bump you off, right now."

George raised a placating palm.

"Take it easy, baby," he said. "Now, Lou—dig 'em up."

Santolo started for the hallway and George nudged Johnny in the ribs with the gun.

"You too," he said. "I gotta keep you in range, buddy."

They went into the dining-room—Santolo first, then Johnny, finally George and Stella.

Santolo ripped off the lace table-cloth which decorated the big oak table.

"In there," he pointed at the table-top.

But George stood, watching him suspiciously.

"Jake," he said. "Get 'em out, Towser—that's a good dog."

Santolo smiled faintly and pulled open the table, with an effort, so that there was a space between the leaves. He reached in a hand and brought out a bundle, tied in tissue paper.

"There's another," he said and leaned over the table again.

George put out a hand for the bundle, ripped off the tissue.

"*Look out!*" screamed Stella.

Santolo's hand emerged from the table leaves with a big automatic that started spitting flame as soon as it reached the level of the table-top.

George winced as the shock of the first bullet smashed his left arm; but he fired carefully, once, twice—emptied all six chambers into the body of the sallow man, which slumped slowly to the floor.

The last shot in the automatic went wild; ricocheted from the steel door-jamb and caught George at about the third vest button.

He said: "Unhhh," coughed queerly and sat down on the floor.

Stella flung herself on the floor beside him; her blonde hair was flecked with little red bubbles from his lips.

Johnny felt of George's heart, saw that the bullet had gone in below the lung. In the inside coat pocket of the detective he found a familiar wallet, which contained an uncashed check.

"He won't die," he said to the sobbing girl, "but he'll probably get a long rest in Leavenworth before he's right again."

"Get a doctor… hurry," she wailed. "He's dying."

"Sure," Johnny said soothingly, as he picked up the phone. "I told him I'd need an ambulance."

But the number he called was police headquarters.

One for the Book

Johnny Hi Gear is an unbidden guest
at a private pineapple party

THE BIG MAN tilted the dull silk hat off a wind-tanned forehead, rested a foot on the brass rail and an elbow on the mahogany:

"How long you been running a carnival gyp, Joey?"

The white mustaches of the old Italian on the other side of the bar bristled, the musty skin flushed darkly and he turned frosty blue eyes in the direction indicated by the ebony cane which the other pointed at the far end of the speakeasy.

"Ha. *Datta* t'ing, you mean? It is nota mine.... I no lika you see it in my place." He glared at the aluminum-painted machine, with its slots and dial and hand-crank, as if it were a dangerous animal.

The man in evening dress fished a slice of orange from the bottom of his glass.

"They're rigged to clip seventy, eighty per cent for the house, aren't they? The suckers don't ask for a break, do they? What the hell?"

The speakeasy proprietor shrugged.

"I don't needa jack so bad. It's a stick-up racket, mister, around men who been drinking. You know what?"

The other chewed the orange, shook his head.

"Lasta week, two deesa bums muscle in here and dump datta junk on my bar. 'Run it and like it,' dey tella me. 'Cut us for feefty a week and you taka de rest yourself.'"

The big man smiled.

"Baloney!"

"I tol''em where dey could stuffa de slot machine... and I kicked da collector out on his pants w'en he try gyp me for first week's rent," said the Italian.

"Watch your step, Joe." The big man climbed into his overcoat. "You don't want to be taking slugs, instead of the machine. Lot of these jack-pot babies are sniffers, you know."

Little Joe Massetti nodded.

"Yellow-bellies w'en dey're off a de stuff and mad dogs w'en dey have a card.... I know, Johnny."

"Well... be seeing you."

"Be good boy, Johnny."

The big man closed the inside door after him and let himself out through the iron-grilled door which led to the areaway. Before he could swing the gate behind him, two figures stepped close beside him from the shadowy gloom under the steps.

"Back up... back up," said one pleasantly.

Johnny hesitated. He could not see either of them clearly... could not be sure whether they carried guns.

"Whassa matt'r. Whass wrong?" he said thickly.

"Go on back, you mug." The other man's voice was a high, piping falsetto. "Reverse it." He put a hand against Johnny's chest, shoved hard.

Several things happened so fast as to be practically simultaneous: Johnny slipped, he swung a short uppercut, his hat skidded off into the slush, something hard jabbed painfully in his stomach and he recognized it for an automatic while he was saying "Hah," quite involuntarily.

He had dropped his cane: now he lifted his arms from his sides and showed gloved palms.

"No need of the broderick," he said, quietly. "And you won't find any heavy dough on me, either... but go ahead." The pleasant voiced one swore savagely and swung a hard flat hand at his face.

"———! This ain't Massetti. This kluck's twice as big as Little Joe—"

He poked the gun lower and Johnny grunted at the hurt.

"Jeeze," squeaked the falsetto. "That's a honey, boss. Nearly give the works to the wrong beezark." He laughed, shrilly. "What we gonna do with him?"

The one with the gun kicked the silk hat to one side, picked up the cane and broke it over his knee.

"Ah, go on, you mug," he snarled at Johnny. "Beat it before I change my mind and plug you."

Johnny started up the three steps to the sidewalk when they pushed him. He sprawled flat in wet snow. Something hit him in the back of the head.... It was the broken cane.

He got to his feet, fighting mad, saw the two figures watching, caught the reflected gleam from the automatic; thought better of it.

He brushed his trousers and limped slowly down the street.

HIS FACE WAS scratched and bleeding, his shins ached, his groin pained fiercely. He was hatless, soaking wet and cold with rage.

But he walked far enough down the block to spot the black sedan with the open windows and softly purring motor. The driver he deduced from a glowing cigarette tip; he could not see his face. The license was sure to be a fake, but he noted the cracked head-lamp, the dented fender and new hub-cap.

That watchful driver meant that whatever was due to happen at Little Joe's would be over in a rush: if Johnny was going to step into that picture he had to do it in a hurry. He turned and limped back towards the speakeasy.

Behind him, gears meshed softly; tires slithered in the snow. The getaway man was going into action.

All Johnny needed was a minute; he counted on uncertainty in the lookout's mind for sixty seconds. As he dived into the areaway, he picked up the broken cane. He shoved the piece with the crook on it, through the scrolled opening in the grille about a foot under the metal plate guarding the latch, held it hard against the knob inside, pressed and pushed upwards slightly and leaned on the gate. There was a click; the door swung open.

He got inside, closed the door as the sedan slid to a stop before Little Joe's place. The driver was on the running-board, as it pulled up.

Johnny paused at the inner door to work his gun free from his shoulder-holster; he put his ear to the wooden panel.

"*Dio Mio!* Notta dat...." Little Joe's voice was hoarse with terror. "I'll pay... for da machine... don't maka me—" The words ended with an unpleasant gurgling sound.

Johnny went in, quietly.

The white-haired old Italian was bent grotesquely backwards over his own bar, his head resting on the brass plate used to drain beer stoppings. A waxy-skinned, pinch-featured thin man behind the mahogany held the white hair in one hand while with the other he attempted to force something that shone of copper between the speakeasy proprietor's clenched teeth.

A blocky, beefy-faced man with lustreless gray eyes and a cruel slit of a mouth stood before Little Joe and twisted his wrists savagely.

"Swallow 'em, punk," sneered the red-faced man, as Johnny got the door open. "Get 'em down. They're only .32s. Good f'r what ails you... cure guaranteed to last. Easier t' chew 'em than have 'em *pumped* into you. This way you last three, four days. Maybe that'll straighten up somea you gees that been high-hattin' us lately." He laughed as Waxy-Face stuck his thumbs into Massetti's jaws and forced them open.

"Up," snapped Johnny. "Way up... quick!"

The man behind the bar let go Little Joe's hair, the Italian slumped to the floor in a faint and the beefy man whirled on his toes like a boxer.

"You?" He spat out a short, astonished sibilant and reached for his pocket.

Johnny put his right arm out low and straight.

"I'll let you have it," he warned.

A blunt-nosed automatic emerged from the stocky man's coat....

Johnny fired at his belt buckle; the man raised his gun slowly.

"Well!" Johnny let go twice more, point blank. He could not miss that chunky chest at eight feet. The man spun halfway round, his mouth opened noiselessly but he got his automatic on a line with Johnny's heart.

Johnny swung to one side, there was a stab of light and something hit him in the shoulder like a sledge-hammer blow. He tried to work the trigger again, heard his gun crash to the floor and realized that his right arm was useless.

The red-faced man took two steps forward and snarled:

"You hadda stick *your* ————damn' nose in. You asked for it, you ——— ——— so..." he took deliberate aim, "here it is."

Johnny ducked, let his knees buckle and rolled as he fell; powder grains stung the side of his face and the sound of the shot was deafening, but he felt no pain. His head crashed into the brass foot-rail, his shoulder lunged into the face of the bar and he wondered what delayed the finishing shot.

...Then he heard the four quick notes of the Klaxon.

"Kippy," shrilled a voice from the other side of the bar. "That's Pete's signal... c'mon... let's scram."

Johnny lay very still: perhaps they would think he was dead.

"We can't leave no trail like this." The thick-set man swore obscenely. "Frisk that wise guy.... I'll go through Massetti."

The waxy-faced one kicked Johnny in the knee, flopped him

over and took his wallet, cigarette case and a watch that Johnny valued above price.

"Hop it up, Kippy," begged the thin man. "C'mon."

Little Joe had recovered, was on his knees, mumbling a prayer in Italian.

"Here you!" Johnny saw the man called Kippy take something like a big black egg from his overcoat and hold it in front of the Italian's eyes. "Here's where you have one on th' house… pineapple flavor."

He pulled the pin and ran to the door; Waxy-Face was already outside.

"You won't crash no more parties, wise guy," snarled Kippy, looking at Johnny from the door. "You c'n go f'r that… that's one for the book."

He tossed the bomb at Johnny and vanished.

ALL JOHNNY COULD think of, during that split second, was that it was a hell of a way to cash in… with his head in a spittoon.

But his muscles flashed into action, even before the black egg which hatched death was out of Kippy's hand; twisting and rolling his body towards the protection of the battered iron safe at the end of the bar. He drew his legs under him, like a falling cat, covered his eyes with his good arm and ducked….

… he was lifted and slammed against the big iron box; the air was a paralyzing burst of searing flame and he lost consciousness.

How long he was out, he never knew; when he first heard the ringing of the concussion in his ears and opened his eyes, he could see nothing and thought, momentarily, that he was blind. Then he smelt the acrid fumes of powder and alcohol—realized that the lights must have been shattered—got a match from his pocket shakily.

Clouds of plaster dust and a rain of splinters and shattered glass obscured the wreckage, but he saw something gruesome on the floor ten feet away—and winced as from a blow. He felt sick and weak, his eyes were blurry and his hands unsteady at lighting the matches… but there was no need of worrying about Little Joe Massetti any more.

He leaned limply against the crazily uprooted bar and rescued a bottle which had not been smashed… it had a Hennessey Three Star label… he cracked off the neck, and let hot fluid pour into his bruised mouth. He wiped his face, wet with perspiration—and shivered. Why he had not been blown to bits like the red, raw thing on the floor there… he did not know.

Presently his ears made out another sound than the high-pitched ringing which echoed and reechoed through his numbed brain—a confused noise of whistles blowing, people shouting, feet pounding on pavements.

Someone was hammering at the front door. In a minute or so the place would be seething with cops and plain-clothes men… but he couldn't wait to see them. He had an appointment with a red-faced man and a coke, and he had to be in shape to keep that date. He couldn't do it in Bellevue, or in the Tombs as a material witness. Even the fact that he was on the confidential list of the Commissioner as an under-cover man wouldn't help him in this jam.

He got some more of the Three Star down and shook his head to clear it. His right hand was wet; he looked down, it was covered with blood. Gritting his teeth he got the hand in his overcoat pocket, with the aid of his left. Then he picked up the gun… there were still three shots left… he remembered.

The noise at the front door had redoubled.

He picked his way over debris, across the horrible thing that had been Little Joe Massetti but five minutes ago, and found what he was looking for: the trap-door to the barrel cellar. Every speake has one.

He lifted the iron ring, tugged and got the trap open. He backed down the beer-soaked stairs just as the iron-grille crashed open and feet hurried along the corridor to the inner door. He dropped the trap above him.

The cellar was pitch-dark, slimy with grease and seepage, close and fetid. He got out a match, lit it and worked his way towards the front of the cellar. There would be a street-level opening somewhere… twice a week the furniture van would pull up and drop fifteen or twenty half barrels of Jersey beer down that opening, after paying the cop-tax of a dollar a barrel.

He located it by the time the emergency patrol and the ambulance pulled up in front of the speakeasy. They would search the cellar in a few minutes, of that he was sure. So he pushed the metal hatch open and looked out; there were a dozen people in the street and two internes getting a stretcher ready. He bit his lips as he thought of getting what was left of Little Joe on a stretcher.

There would be a bluecoat in the area and more on the way. He had to bluff it out now, if he was to make it good.

"Jeeze!" He shouted to one of the bystanders, a negro musician bound Harlemwards after his night-club duties. "What happened… hey?"

"Still blew up, boss." The black man hurried on, anxious to be the first to give information. "Wop runs a still—that's what they say, boss."

"Crying out loud," said Johnny. "Scared me so I fell off a pile of barrels. Here... gimme a hand; I've got a game wrist."

The negro reached down to the loading platform, heaved him flat on the sidewalk. Johnny got to his feet, dizzily.

"Lordy, boss... you look like you was inside that still. The wop's croaked... they gone in for him."

"I'm kayo. Just scratched up a little. I gotta report this... I'm supposed to be watchman...."

Johnny thought the explanation was pretty cockeyed, but he couldn't dope out anything better... and he started down the street. Curious eyes followed him—suspicious whispers followed him... but none of them belonged to uniforms, so Johnny sauntered on casually.

He turned up his coat collar to hide the dirt and blood on his collar and shirt.

Fifty feet from the Avenue he looked back at the gathering crowd—and saw a black sedan creeping slowly along behind him, close to the curb. It had a cracked head-lamp and a dented fender.

He broke into a run, pulling out his gun. At the corner is a church; the car caught up to him as he dodged into the blackness of the chapel door. Orange blades of light knifed through the sedan's windows.... Stone chipped from the portals and lead rang against bronze doors.

Johnny steadied himself, fired three times from a crouch as the car passed. The black car swerved suddenly, hurdled the opposite curb and smashed head on into an iron railing; finally flopping on its side.

TWO MEN GOT out of the rear of the car and ran around the corner; one was a short stocky figure, the other thin and taller. The driver of the car did not move; looked as if he were asleep at the wheel. Traffic whistles shrilled; down the block behind him a motorcycle stuttered into rapid-fire.

Johnny tried the church door. It was unlocked. He wandered through the high-vaulted chapel, sat in one of the pews for a minute to pull his shaken nerves together.

Voices came to him from the dim, quiet vault above him... then he realized, with a start, that those voices were real. Here, in the church, close to him. He dropped on his knees and crouched low.

"... all covered... if we can smoke this high-hat baby... what's his name?"

It was Kippy. Johnny began crawling on one hand and a knee, but he kept his gun in the hand on which he rested his weight and went softly.

"John Hiram Gear... Hotel Metropole... what a break..." said the other, shrill voice. Johnny cursed through his teeth; they had taken his wallet—he had forgotten that. In his wallet were cards, papers and... a sweet roll of the ready. Well, he had to get them before they got him... and he had been planning to do just that, for Little Joe's sake, as well as his own....

He reached the door of the anteroom, through which one might have access to the great hall of the church... and the Avenue. The voices had ceased. He got his head around the corner of the door, his gun lifted.

The place was but faintly lighted, but he could see that it was empty. He got to his feet in time to hear the sound of a gently closing door. He walked unsteadily through the minister's room, down the long, carpeted aisle past the high pulpit, to the high, paneled doors.

By the time he reached the Avenue, there was only a cruising yellow to be seen... and a knot of curious men being shoved back from the ruin of the black sedan.

Johnny hailed the taxi.

"Metropole... in a rush, buddy," he said.

"My ———! fella!" The driver turned around in his seat. "You been *hurt*. Better let me take you to a hospital."

"I said... the Metropole. And snap it up. If I wanted to go to a hospital I'd—"

There was a backfire noise and the side window of the cab made a queer tinkling sound: a thousand little cracks radiated from the round hole a foot from Johnny's head.

"Now... will you step on it?" Johnny swore harshly... the driver galvanized into activity, jerked his clutch in and the car leaped forward.

"Listen... you," he said in a scared voice, as he wheeled the machine around a corner by inches. I gotta damn' good mind to take you around to Forty-seventh Street. By jeeze... I think that's where you belong... you look as if you'd mixed up in something...."

Johnny worked his gun free once more, kept it where the jockey wouldn't see it and chuckled:

"Don't be a sap. If there was anything wrong with me, would I be asking you to take me to the Metropole? I live there... you can check me up with the doorman. And if you get me there fast, so's the house doc can fix these scratches of mine..." he gritted his teeth as his arm jolted against the rocking side of the taxi... "there's a ten-spot in it, for you." There was something less negotiable in it, if he refused, Johnny thought, grimly.

"Say, get me right... I'm no yellow-belly," said the driver. "But I don't hire out to be shot at... and somebody's got to pay for that glass."

Johnny grunted. They were pulling up before the hotel now.

"Coupla stick-up gees, that was. They tried to put the stopper on me once before, tonight... that's all there is to it." Johnny tried to make his voice convincing.

"Oh, yeah?" The driver was skeptical. "And don't forgetsis... I gotta make a report on this... you better be on the up-an'-up, or they'll be puttin' the finger on you." He stopped the car with a jerk.

The doorman was there. Johnny got out of the car, painfully.

"What's my name, Timmy?" He grinned at the big, jovial, uniformed Irishman.

"Ye don't even know th' name of yourself, is it?" The doorman came closer. "And have ye been hittin' th' high spots, th' night, Mister Gear?"

"Hell," said the driver. "I thought I'd seen your pan before... you're Johnny Hi Gear, the big dice an' card boy, uh?"

Johnny said: "Lend me a ten-spot, Timmy."

Timmy looked wonderingly at the bruised face, the shattered window and the coat-sleeve stuck in the right-hand pocket.

"Sure... sure," he hastened. "You better git inside, Mister Gear.... I'll take care of the taxi."

"Give him a tenner," said Johnny from the revolving doors. "And much obliged."

He got up to his room, with no more attention than the surprised glances of early morning scrub-women cleaning the lobby, the proffered assistance of a bell-hop and the unexpressed curiosity of the elevator-boy.

When he got to his room, he locked the door, got out a cigarette and sat on the bed beside the phone.

"Let me talk to Doc Benter," he said to the sleepy phone operator. "Hello, Doc… this is Johnny Gear. C'mon over. And bring your kit of tools…. Oh, I had an argument with a telephone pole," he finished with a chuckle. He eased himself down to wait.

Three minutes later there was a knock on the door.

He opened it.

"Positively my last appearance," said Kippy. "Get back… go on."

THE CIGARETTE WAS between Johnny's lips. He took a drag on it, blew the smoke in Kippy's face and walked slowly backward. The other followed closely; shut the door and locked it.

"We was expectin' you to buzz th' house-doc," he said in a flat, brittle tone. "So little Egghead is sittin' on Benter's belly, right now." He backed Johnny into the armchair before the little writing table, put a hand against his chest and shoved him to a sitting position. "Anyhow, you ain't gonna need no doc."

Johnny said: "Hell you say."

Kippy reached over his shoulder, got the desk drawer open and pulled out paper and pen.

"You're gonna go bye-bye, sucker. But I'll deal you a break… you can pick y'r exit."

"That's nice." Johnny thought he knew what the letter-paper meant.

"Yeah. If you act wise, you can take a punch on the chin and let the bulls pick you up f'r the Massetti kill. Just write a little note right now telling 'em how you happened to bump him off with one 'f these Dago footballs… make it plenty strong, too. Then…."

Johnny grinned.

"—Then you put a rod in my chest and let go—that it?"

Kippy lifted gross eyebrows in mock amazement.

"Don't be like that. Why should I trig you when you're a swell out f'r me an' Egghead? Huh? Be your age."

Johnny tapped the pen with his left hand.

"No sale. I can't use my right mitt, at all."

Kippy kicked viciously; his heavy boot caught Johnny in the ankle and he cried out, involuntarily.

"Use your left," snarled the beefy-faced man. "Or I don't give a damn what you use. But write that note, now… or take a drag on this…" he snatched the cigarette out of Johnny's mouth and jammed his automatic savagely against Johnny's teeth.

Johnny rolled with the blow, closed his eyes, said "nnnh-h-h" dully and fell over on the floor. Kippy gave him the boot in the ribs, but Johnny didn't stir.

Kippy swore in disgust.

"Out like a light… well, baby, I'll bring you back to life." He went into the bathroom and ran the water. Then he came back, got an arm under Johnny's head and poured ice-water down his neck.

Johnny sat up, dizzily.

Kippy was squatting near him, a glass in his left hand, the gun in his right. The little, pale eyes were sneering.

"Come out of it, delicate. You gotta letter t' write. Don't forget it."

Johnny saw something on the carpet, it glittered faintly in the darkness of the rich maroon velvet.

"Yeah." He spoke thickly. "Sure." He leaned forward, got his left hand over the object and added: "You'll have to lift me."

Kippy said: "Get up yourself, you ———! And get up *now*."

Johnny lurched to his feet, swung a little and tossed something out of the open window.

Kippy lifted the automatic menacingly.

"What the hell… what'd you chuck outta that window? What was it?" He took a step forward, his head lowered, his eyes glittering.

Johnny sat down, reached for the pack of cigarettes on the desk.

"Mind if I smoke?" He spoke very politely.

Kippy showed uneven, gold-capped teeth.

"What—was—that—you—threw?" he said, spacing his words carefully.

Johnny flipped open his lighter.

"My life insurance," he said, easily. "The key to this room." Kippy's finger tightened on the trigger and Johnny tried to keep his voice calm and steady. "You won't want to be found in here with a hundred and eighty pounds of first-degree evidence, will you, Kippy?"

The stubby finger relaxed its pressure on the trigger, the gun dropped muzzle-down and the stocky man backed towards the other side of the room. Then he whirled quickly and tried the door; he had locked it himself… and now there was no way to get out.

"All right… all right," he said. "Don't think that'll keep you from takin' the full dose, Mister Johnny Hi Gear…. I been in tighter spots than this, an' I'm still pickin' 'em up an' layin' 'em down."

He reversed the gun, walked deliberately to Johnny's chair and clubbed him twice, where the bullet had hit his right shoulder.

Johnny thought he was going to pass out of the picture for good, but he managed to keep a grip on his reeling senses. Kippy smashed the Colt against the side of Johnny's face as a final caress, went to the phone and called: "Doc Benter, please."

"Hello… Egghead? Listen close, kid. Johnny's done a fadeaway… and I want doc to come right up… but Johnny locked th' door before he fainted. Get th' extra key from the desk and jump right up…. Right?"

He hung up.

"You got just as long as it takes Egghead to beat it up here, to get ready for the big dive, mug. I had just enough of y'r ——— dam'…."

He looked in astonishment at the bed, across the room—a lazy coil of thick, white smoke was curling from the floor like mist.

Johnny spoke from the floor, where he had dived when his lighter had ignited the edge of the woolly blankets, the sheet and mattress:

"Think it over, hard-boiled. You're in bad enough, as it is."

He threw one of his shoes through the window.

KIPPY STARED.

The cloth smoked furiously; oily waves of thick gray fumes oozed to the window level, eddied around the ceiling.

Then the man across the room ran to the bathroom. Johnny got to his knees, used his left hand to yank the curtains from their wooden cornice and throw them on the blazing blankets.

Kippy dashed out of the bathroom, panic in his fish-like eyes; his voice throaty with fear:

"Jeeze... you wanta burn us t'death? You wanta..." he spilled half a tumbler of water three feet from the blaze. The smoke was quite dense now.

Johnny got to his feet; grabbed the phone and hollered: "Fire... fire!" loudly. Then he left the receiver off the hook and said: "The John Laws will be here before your pal, Egghead, makes the grade. What about it, Kippy?"

"————!" The other screamed in rage and fright. "I'll fix your works, you crazy...."

There was a knocking at the door.

"Who's inside? Who's in there?" said a voice. It was not Egghead.

"Get the police!" yelled Johnny. "And bring an extinguisher."

"Open the door... what's burning?" The voice was getting excited.

Kippy gulped in the fog-like coils of thick, acrid smoke. He slipped the safety on his automatic and stuck it under the bed, fired once, twice. Then he put a bullet through the pillows... another through the foot of the bed.

Johnny crawled past him through the smoke to the bathroom, got inside and closed the door, turned the lock. There was a ventilator which kept the air a little clearer; outside the curtains had blazed up... one of the chair seats was beginning to burn.

Feet were padding up and down the corridor; voices came over the transom in fragmentary clarity:

"... Sent in the alarm... break it down... something about police... that's Johnny Hi Gear's room...."

Johnny ran water in the bowl; drank a glass of ice-water. His arm and shoulder were one throbbing ache. His face was swollen and bleeding… his lips cut and bruised. One ankle was knifing him with pain.

Ping! The medicine-cabinet mirror tinkled to the washbowl in silvery, shattered bits of glass. Kippy was trying to write him off the books.

He stepped into the bathtub, turned on the cold shower and watched a row of little holes appear in the panels of the door. Concrete chipped from the walls and metal rang loudly, but he was untouched.

Crash! Someone was trying to break down the door. Why didn't the fools get the duplicate key, Johnny wondered. Then he realized that it was Kippy who was trying to smash his way through to freedom.

The falling rain of cool water cleared the air a bit—he could breathe more easily now. He sniffed; there was a pungent odor in the smoke… he recognized it for extinguisher-fluid… they must be putting it in through the transom.

Then someone was hammering on the bathroom door:

"Open up… come out of there, you fool… do you hear? Come out… the fire's over."

It was a new voice and Johnny turned the lock and stepped out. Water dripped off him in pools; his clothing was plastered to his skin and he could only stand erect with an effort.

A smallish, black-haired man in a derby hat and a dark suit stood outside the bathroom door; the room was full of men seen vaguely through the wreaths of smoke which drifted out through the wide-flung windows.

"Well… maybe you'll tell us what it's all about?"

"Get him?" Johnny started stripping off wet clothing, grunted with the reaction from his shoulder. The corridor was crowded with curious guests, bell-hops, maids, policemen.

The houseman gave him a hand with his soaking coat.

"Boy! You're plugged, for fair. What happened?"

"Did you nail him?" Johnny wanted to know, wringing water from his trousers, kicking off his remaining shoe. The walls of the room were smoke-stained, discolored; the carpet was a mess. Curtains and draperies had been torn down, pictures smashed… and the bed smelled like burning goat-hair.

One of the harness bulls stepped in:

"That bird… the one with the burned face… was he the one who was shooting off that rod? My ———! man! You're *hurt!*"

Johnny swore softly as he got into a dry dressing gown; he had to lift his right arm into the sleeve.

"Some," he admitted. "That's a present from the… gee you let walk away… suppose he's halfway… to Albany by now." Talking was painful.

"Oh, yeah?" The bluecoat was scowling. "Listen, fella. That playmate of yours is with Sergeant Connolly, right now. At the doctor's. He got burned, half the skin is off his face. But he's where we can put the bracelets on him; if he's the rod that worked on you… we'll be havin' fun."

Johnny said: "Oh! At the doctor's? With a sergeant? We better snap down there, *pronto.* Maybe… your officer will need the doc… unless…."

… It was a curious procession, that pell-mell rush down the two flights of stairs: half-dressed women, timorous bell-hops, plain-clothes men… and Johnny.

The door to Doc Benter's room was open.

Sergeant Connolly lay on his face, his arms outstretched. The house physician was in the closet, trussed up with belts and cords. Connolly had been hit from behind, with a blackjack. The doctor was unconscious, but unhurt.

On the desk, under a green-shaded lamp, lay a silver hypodermic.

THEY UNTIED THE doctor, gave him whiskey and let him talk. The sergeant didn't respond so easily.

"… Look out for the thin one," mumbled the physician. "He's full of cocaine…. Hello, Johnny. You look bad… who's the policeman?" They got the story from him, in bits. Egghead and Kippy had jumped him, after gaining entrance to his room in the guise of patients. Kippy had departed: Egghead had tried one means of crude torture after another until the doctor had consented to reveal the small stock of drugs he had. Then the thin man had stoked up… he was as dangerous as a mad dog, thought Benter.

The officer came to, after a minute or so, but it was another five before he could explain.

"Had this heavy-set one in front of me"… he put a hand to his aching head and rested his elbows on knees, dispiritedly. "Didn't know which one was the doc… he got back of me, for a second, and gave me the tap… where'd they go?"

Nobody knew.

Cops ran around in circles; bandages and plaster were put in action; Johnny's arm got attention; telephones went hot-wire with overwork—but Kippy and the Egghead had vanished into thin air.

"You better get a good, long sleep, Johnny." Benter was finishing the dressing on his arm. "I suppose the precinct will want to nurse you in Bellevue, as a material witness… but I can stall 'em off for a day, maybe. Urgent danger… infection… you know."

"Thanks a lot," said Johnny. "I don't want to be cooped up, right now. I got things to do."

"You better not do 'em," growled Benter. "You mean hunting for that couple of thugs? Lay off—leave it to the cops."

"They'll never lam outta here." The bluecoat who had been left by the sergeant's orders, as a guard over Johnny, was heavily confident.

Johnny said: "Yeah?" and got a hooker of rye inside his belt. The cop took one, with him.

"They know these babies," nodded the patrolman. "Kippy Minzer… he's got a record like Legs Di-mond… out on parole now, he is… Thanks." The second glass followed the first in close formation… then a third.

"Slot machine was his racket?" Johnny inquired as he filled the cop's glass for the fifth time.

"You know it." The officer unbuttoned the top button of his coat. "Them slot machines, now. They're lousy… Jeeze, this's good stuff." He held his glass to the light admiringly.

"Have another." Johnny got amber liquid right up to the brim, nodded affably, though his arm hurt like hell.

"Mind 'f I do," said the policeman.

"Warms you up," Johnny filled up more glasses and Benter, refusing one, watched him curiously. Two more buttons came free on the blue coat. Then the officer stepped out of the room for a minute.

"Got a gun, doc?"

"Sure, Johnny… but I wouldn't let you have it, shape you're in."

"Hell. Self-protection, doc. This dumb bunny in uniform would be about as much use in a jam as nothing at all. He's cocked, now."

"Mm, huh." The doctor went over to a closet, took something off the shelf. He laid it on the desk beside Johnny.

"Don't say I gave it to you. It's a .32… and all ready to work. But you pinched it, if anything happens. I never gave it to you.…"

Johnny got the gun in his left dressing gown pocket and grinned.

"That's *my* story, too."

"What you goin' to do, now you've got it?"

"Listen, doc." Johnny got over near the door, stood with his back to the wall. "I'm the only witness to a pineapple-throwing that these two worked early this morning. The man that went out was a good friend of mine. They tried to get me, too… but I got a break. I'm going to turn 'em up, before they turn *me* up. They came into the Metropole to put the tag on me… and again I had some luck. So.…"

"Maybe you won't be so fortunate the third time."

Johnny said: "I'd thought about that." The patrolman came in the room, bleary-eyed. Johnny edged through the door without waiting to hear what explanation the doctor might give. He was at the turn of the corridor when the door opened and the bluecoat bellowed:

"Hey, you. Hey, Mister Gear. *Hey!* You can't run away like that.…"

It was an effort to climb the two flights of stairs. He was short of breath when he reached the end of the corridor leading to his room.

There was a big closet five feet away and Johnny paid it no attention, but the minute of waiting to get his breath was the margin between death and life, for....

...The door opened, an inch at a time, the aperture away from him. Noiselessly he got to the stair-door and stepped into the well. Through a half-inch crack he could see Kippy, sidling along the wall towards the door of the room he had left only an hour before. He tried the door, called softly, found no one on guard and went in.

Johnny's first impulse was to follow—then he remembered Egghead. That coke-eater would be nearby... but where. Johnny thought he knew. He stepped to the closet, got his gun out and said:

"Come out, Egghead... and come out backward, too. When you've got the door open, chuck your rod on the floor."

The closet door opened slowly.

JOHNNY SAW A thin back, jabbed his .32 at it and heard something drop on the floor. He picked it up by the trigger guard, stuffed it in a side pocket, with his left hand.

"Ever hear how a man dies with a hole in his kidneys?" Johnny was walking Egghead down the hall, keeping close behind him, prodding him with the revolver. "Takes a week or ten days... they say it's the most terrible way to kick in, that there is."

"You got me wrong, mister. I never hurt no one. Not me. You got me wrong."

"I've got you *right*, Egghead. You're going to stay that way. And—unless you want me to drill two holes in your kidneys, you'll tell Kippy to come out, when we get to my room. Ask him nice and quiet. Say I've gone to the hospital. Make it sound natural... or else...."

Egghead started to turn around. Johnny drew the gun back six inches and lunged at the small of the thin man's back. It straightened him up like a galvanic shock.

They halted in front of Johnny's room.

"Do your stuff," whispered Johnny.

Egghead started to swing his right arm, backward and forward, just a little, but he said nothing.

"Stick your arms up. Clasp those mitts behind your neck. Go on... or I'll give it to you right now. That's better. Now *talk!*"

Egghead muttered something unintelligible.

"When I count three... I'll pull the trigger," Johnny said softly. "One, two, thr—"

"Kippy!" Egghead's voice was shrill.

"You lousy fink... what you doing out in that hall?" The man inside was sore.

"Boss! We better scram. That mug's not comin' back today. They took him to the hospital."

"Shut up. Do what I told you, or I'll come out there and blow you apart—hear me?"

Johnny put his mouth close to Egghead's ear:

"Tell him to go to hell... you're going to beat it," he whispered.

Kippy said: "You going?"

"You go to hell... I'm gonna scram." Egghead's tone was not defiant, but the words carried sufficient surprise, for the door opened.

Kippy looked into the muzzle of Johnny's gun and lowered his head, as a bull does when it makes its charge.

"I'll be a ——— ———," he said. "You double-crossing dope, you…."

"That'll be all," said Johnny. "Get up those mitts."

"He made me, boss," whimpered Egghead.

"Yeah?" Kippy's hand went to his left shoulder and Johnny fired. Not at the chest, not at the stomach. Right between the eyes.

There was a simultaneous spurt of hot flame from Kippy's gun.

Egghead murmured: "Ah!" in astonishment and buckled at the knees.

"You've got a bullet-proof vest, Kippy," said Johnny. "And I had this snowbird, for my bullet-proof. That's an even break."

Kippy could not hear him. He lay, face down, over the threshold of the wrecked room. A thin stream of dark red ran away from his forehead like a piece of cord.

The policeman he had slipped came pounding down the hall.

"Say, you," he bellowed, belligerently.

"Pipe down. Get a little sense, copper. This is a break for you, if you use your head. You've been in on a cleanup—if I say so."

"Well…" The officer was dubious.

"Get a load of this," said Johnny in an undertone. "You came up to my room with me… an errand, see… and they shot it out with us. You get a rating, account of this, if you're smart."

"Sure," breathed the cop. "I make you, mister. You sure are a busy little powder-burner, ain't you?"

Johnny felt very tired.

"I'm going back to doc's room. I need a good double-order of sleep. But don't forget what I told you. How it happened."

"I'll play ball," said the man in uniform. "What'll I do with this…" he turned Egghead over. The coke's face was pasty-gray and his lips were blue.

Johnny looked at the wet spot on the thin man's vest.

"He might be patched up for the chair," he said, finally. "Anyway… he's got a chance."

"I'll take him in," said the cop.

"Hell, yes." Johnny walked towards the stairs, through the curious crowd. "He's one for the book, all right."

Starita Takes a Rumble

Johnny Hi Gear collects a bet in red

THE MAN IN the rink-side seat wore a camel's hair coat, a much darker coat of Florida sunburn and an air of quiet expectancy. Most of the crowd in the Garden were standing, yelling, cheering… but the tanned figure sitting by the blue line lit a cigarette calmly.

A Bluejay wingman dodged, eluded a poke-check by a skilful dribble and flashed down the scarred ice….

Bud Lutin, burly Eagle defense man, dug in his blades and lunged with a stocky shoulder at the speeding figure. There was a sound like a sledge-hammer hitting soft wood—the Bluejay hit the ice ear first, slewed to the sideboards and got shakily to his knees. Jerry Broach, the Eagle goalie, came out of the cage, blocked the puck and shot it out of the danger zone.

The Jay center sprinted, blocked and recovered the rubber; turned at a sharp angle and shot for the net.

Jerry put up a padded glove, slapped the puck down. It wobbled crazily a few feet in front of him. Three sticks slashed viciously for its possession. The Jay center caught the disk on the heel of his stick, lifted hard.

Jerry was in a spot. He had been wangled out of position when the mêlée in front of the cage began, had fallen full length on the ice in an effort to smother a scoring shot. He got one hand on the ice and raised his head—the puck thudded against his chin… rebounded halfway across the rink.

The Garden roared. Bud Lutin made a snap recovery, ran down the sideboards and took a long shot, high and fast.

The red eye in the Bluejay cage winked cheerily; a bell rang sharply... and the great arena became a wild maelstrom of noise.

"Sweet work, Jerry," said the man in the buff coat. "That's using your head."

He chuckled at the screeching galleries, grinned admiringly at the snow coated figure of the little goalie and made his way out of the crowd boiling from the Garden. He went a block north on Eighth, turned left and rang a bell beside a freshly painted green door.

The door opened on a chain; a brick-red Irish face peered through the six-inch opening.

"F'r the luvva gawd."

The chain rattled.

"Where the divvil y' been, Johnny? C'min.... C'min."

"Hello, Mick. How's things, you fat ape?"

"So-so, Johnny. Jeeze, it's swell t' lamp your mug again. I heard you was mussed up plenty."

"I was, Mike. Make it a sour... and lay on it heavy."

"Right, Johnny. Ya got yaself a dose of lead poisonin', din' ya? Ya'll get yaself bumped off one 'f these days."

"Well... here's dirt on the coffin, Mick."

"Ya been outta the pichure a long time, big boy."

"Well, here I am, fit as a fiddle."

"An' ready for trouble, huh?"

"The old gag, Mick. That's the way it goes."

"It'll go that way once too often, Johnny.... Evenin', Mister Starita."

Johnny turned slowly.

"Hawzit, Mick... cripes' sake. Johnny Hi Gear!"

"Not a moving picture, Ciro."

"———! Thought you was pushin' up th' daisies."

"A lot of people get fooled that way, Ciro."

"Yeah? What'll you have, pal?"

"I'm taking only one—and I have it."

"You see that game at th' Garden?" Starita's voice was cordial but his eyes were brightly suspicious.

"A great game." Johnny sipped his sour thoughtfully.

"You're tellin' me?" Ciro Starita laughed with his mouth. "I pick up five gees on that flock of Eagles. That is, unless th' Mick, here, loses th' envelope?"

His beady eyes appraised the bartender.

The Irishman went to the battered safe at the end of the room, swung the door and pulled out a metal drawer. He brought back an envelope, put it in front of the swarthy man.

"It's all there, Mister Starita."

"Thanks, Mick." Starita pulled out a gold-edged wallet, thumbed some yellows, tossed one on the wet mahogany. "For y'r trouble."

Johnny said: "Who was sucker enough to pick the Jays for five grand?"

Starita's mouth made another smile.

"You figure the locals are hot?"

Johnny stirred his drink with a swizzle stick.

"Sweetest damn' bunch of talent in the league, Starita. Fast, tough and smart."

"Like to put a little on th' line for their next go?" The Italian's voice was like olive oil. "Tomorrow night?"

"Against the Condors? Now who would be dummy enough...."

"I would, Johnny. I'm just that dumb."

"Odds?"

"Five'll get you three… if you think the Eagles are aces."

"And for how much?" Johnny asked.

Starita cleared his throat, straightened his tie.

"Say, fifty to thirty."

"Thousand?" Johnny asked slowly.

Starita nodded, his eyes glittering.

Johnny murmured: "It sounds like a nice bet. I'll take it."

Starita had another highball, added a pile of crisp bills to those the bartender had passed him.

They added up to the thirty thousand. He looked inquiringly, a little sarcastically at Johnny.

Johnny reached nonchalantly into a pocket, withdrew a flat billfold from which he took a sheaf of bills that were also crisp. He ruffled them slowly before the eyes of the Italian. They totaled fifty grand. Starita sighed and turned to his highball, concealing from both Johnny and the bartender the sudden hard, almost panicky look that grew in his dark eyes.

Starita had tried a bluff, and it was called. He couldn't run out now; but he would have to find an out or take his medicine; for Johnny's long end was good.

What Starita did not know, or anyone else along the Main Stem for that matter, was that Johnny, special under-cover man for the Commissioner himself, working solely among the big gamblers, always went heeled for just such an opportunity.

"I think I'll buy me a brewery with that jack," Starita murmured, "and keep you stocked with real Pilsener, Mick."

"Yeah?" The bartender was not enthusiastic.

"Don't put down a binder for that brewery until this time

tomorrow. Your foot might slip, Starita." Johnny grinned casually.

"It has," admitted the Italian. "But what the hell… it's only money."

"Nobody's money, until after the game," agreed Johnny.

Starita put out a moist brown palm.

"Gladda see ya back on the Stem, pal. Makes things seem lively again."

"I'll be getting around." Johnny took the Italian's hand and squeezed it hard.

Starita went out softly.

THE BARTENDER PUT the chain back on the door, came back to the cash register and swore in short sibilants.

"Ain't you wise that mugg is a double-crossin' son of a louse, Johnny? You musta gone soft, bein' sick an' all that. Somebody oughta change y'r di'pers."

Johnny frowned into his glass.

"Okey, Mick. Play nursie. But little Johnny isn't ready for the paresis ward yet."

"Oh, no?"

"I know that wop. I hate his guts. But that doesn't mean I can't take his money and like it."

"He'll frame ya."

"He'll try." Johnny dug out a pack of cigarettes, got one going and blew smoke into his glass. "Baseball, sure. Fix the pitcher. Fights—a cinch."

"It ain't no trick to bribe one 'f them stumble bums. Everybody's doin' it...."

"Wrestling?"

"Hah... ya don't even hafta fix *them* cookies. They frame themselves."

Johnny grinned: "Horse racing?"

"Jeeze." The Irishman spat his disgust. "They don't run nothin' but regattas no more. Try an' find one that's on th' level."

Johnny spun a half-dollar on the bar.

"So you think fixing a hockey game wouldn't be so tough, eh?"

"You could get next the officials, Johnny. A penalty at th' wrong spot would wreck any team, huh?"

"Who's got money enough to crook up the boys they've got in the Garden refereeing and umpiring?"

"Rockefeller, maybe. That's right, them babies are on th' up an' up."

Johnny got to the door.

"Say." The bartender held a towel in his extended hand. "What about th' goalie? He's th' lad who could do it."

The big man chuckled.

"A bull's-eye, Mick. A goalie could throw a game as easy as some of these jocks pull a horse… and nobody would be wise."

"Yeah. Sure."

"But listen, you fat ape…."

"What?"

"Keep the old mush closed, eh?"

"I'm a clam, Johnny. S'long."

"So long, Mick."

Johnny got back to the Garden as the lights were being extinguished; crashed past a uniformed guard on the Forty-ninth Street side with a line about "press stuff" and walked down a long cement corridor to a door marked with battered black letters:

Continental Exhibitions, Inc.
Private

He opened the door:

"Hi there, Doogan…."

Two men were sitting in swivel-chairs. The tall one with his feet on the flat-top looked like a Gloucester fishing-captain; lean, hard, brown and shrewd. The other, a short, squat man with pink cheeks, a black mustache and friendly blue eyes, tongued his panatella to one side of his mouth:

"By all that's holy—*Johnny!*"

Johnny showed teeth genially:

"Just back, Doog… am I butting in?"

The plump one climbed out of his chair.

"Cure for sore eyes, Johnny. Know Drury, here?"

"Pleasure," Johnny murmured to the bronzed man.

"Glad to make your acquaintance, Mister Gear," drawled Drury. "Heard plenty about you… mostly bad. Doogan and I were just reckoning our losses to date. Sit down."

Doogan chuckled: "Drury's the angel, Johnny. Anything less than forty per cent net is bankruptcy to him. Sit down. Something on y'r mind?"

Johnny sat on the edge of a desk.

"A little something, maybe. You got a honey of a hockey team, Doog."

The manager blew cigar smoke towards the ceiling, waited.

"I saw them take the Jays tonight," Johnny said quietly. "They're hot. You can split that playoff dough right now."

Both men looked puzzled.

Johnny went on: "I like 'em so well… that I put down a little bet on 'em. To beat the Condors tomorrow night."

"Want us to guarantee it?" Drury said in a bored tone.

"It's not small time, this bet. And it's with a rather unreliable specimen." Johnny lit a cigarette.

"You're not welching or anything, are you?" Drury scowled.

"Loosen up, Johnny." Doogan was curious. "You've bet dough on us. So what? Why all the high pressure?"

Johnny said: "Could a hockey game be framed?"

Drury stood up, moved close.

"Not by this club, you cheap chiseler—"

Johnny held up a protesting palm.

Doogan cut in: "You got him wrong, Drury. Johnny's on the level. But what in hell are you driving at—"

"Just this." Johnny leaned forward. "I've planted fifty grand on tomorrow's game… and I think there's something screwy about it."

"Fifty grand? And I called you cheap!" Drury grunted.

Doogan snapped: "You're cuckoo, Johnny. Nobody could pull a phoney in a hockey game… it couldn't be done."

Johnny looked thoughtful.

"How about a two-time goalie… one that could be reached. Could he miss a few saves, eh?"

Drury stepped forward threateningly…. "Listen… you get the hell and gone out of here or—"

"I'm not thinking of Jerry Broach, Drury. I've known Jerry since he was knee high to a shin guard. I'd bank my last dime on him. He's square and the gamest little goalie in the league."

Doogan looked worried.

"Then what's eating you?"

"Just suppose," Johnny said slowly, "that an… well, say an accident—happened, so's Jerry couldn't put on the pads tomorrow. Would it help your chances?"

"Cripes, Johnny," Doogan growled. "You're always taggin' along after some stink or other. Jerry's okey. What could keep him from taking the net tomorrow?"

"I don't know, Doog. But… just in case?"

Drury sat down; eyed Johnny warily.

"Why, we'd play Mullan. He's our best spare. Not so keen… but good enough to lick the Condors. Say, if you're crazy enough to sock down fifty thousand bones on one hockey go… don't sob on my shirt…."

Johnny smiled slowly.

"Fair enough. Fair enough. And don't you boys yelp about not being warned. You've had the tipoff. Well… be good."

JOHNNY CROSSED THE avenue, found a booth, twiddled a dial.

"Mrs. Broach. Jerry home yet? Not yet?"

"He isn't home.... Who's this calling?"

"Friend of Jerry's, Mrs. Broach. Know where I'd find him now?"

"Well, I don't know. He usually goes to Sansome's for a bite... but he usually gets in before this. I'm sort of worried...."

Johnny said not to be worried and "thanks" and hung up.

He got out of the drug-store, flagged a Yellow, drove to the Metropole Garage and climbed into the eight-cylinder job which fitted the key on his ring. He hit the greens all the way to Central Park, shot up to One Hundred and Tenth, swung into Convent and made seventy on the Speedway. He kept the accelerator to the floor, crossing Dyckman to Broadway's intersection with Riverside Drive; parked half a block farther where red neon letters announced: *For epicures*—SANSOME'S *the famous*. The street seemed deserted.

Johnny swung plate-glass doors, shook his head at a red-haired check girl and grabbed the headwaiter.

"Jerry Broach here?"

The waiter took his time; smoothed his hair, fiddled with his mustache and said:

"Don't know him. Might be here. I couldn't say."

Johnny's lips tightened.

"Get this, grease-ball. No horse from you. You damn' well know Jerry... he's a regular here. And you damned well know whether he's been in or not. Now take your choice."

"Choice of what, hard guy?"

"Me... or the dicks. I might give you a slap in the puss...

but they'll whale you with a rubber hose. Now quick... who'll you talk to?"

The waiter's eyes smoldered with anger; he moistened thick lips with the tip of his tongue.

"Like that, eh?"

"Just like that."

"Why didn't you say so? I thought maybe you was one of them process servers."

Johnny gripped the front of the waiter's dickey, yanked him close and whispered:

"Spit it out, before I sock you. Where's Jerry?"

"Gone."

"Where?"

"Dunno. With a coupla fellers. Ten, fifteen minutes ago. Honest mister... I don't know a thing about it."

Johnny shoved him heavily against the cashier's desk.

"Those muggs come *in* with him?"

"No, sir. They called for him. He was havin' a steak with Mister Starita.... Jeeze... don't hit me!"

"Where's that wop?"

The other backed against the cigar case, shielded his face with one hand and nodded towards the booths in the rear of the café.

Johnny went back, past glass cases of roast ham and bologna, potato salad and herrings, past a candy counter and a pastry cabinet....

"Hi there, pal."

Starita waved a flabby palm.

"Looking for you, Ciro."

"That so? Well, here I am.... Wanna cuppa Java, Johnny?"

"Where's Jerry?"

"Jerry Broach? You're asking me? I just happened to bump into him—"

"You didn't happen to bump him off, did you, Starita?"

"Be your age. Then a coupla lads breeze in, give him the high sign… and he drifts out."

Johnny sat down, lit a cigarette without taking his eyes from the Italian's.

"Ciro, you ————! permit me to give you a tip."

"Bein' friendly, Johnny?"

"If anything should happen to Jerry between now and tomorrow night… anything unpleasant… I'll be looking for you, Starita."

The Italian lost his air of cordiality for an instant.

"You tryin' t' make me responsible for Jerry Broach? Nerts to you."

Johnny blew smoke into the swarthy face.

"I'm just telling you. You'll be S.O.L. if anything happens to Jerry."

"G'wan, tinhorn. Scramola."

"You'll get your hair curled in that hot seat at Ossining yet, wop."

Starita picked up his cup, swirled the dregs lazily.

"You shoot off your face too much, Johnny. I think you're just a pan of mush."

"Think I'm soft, hey?"

"Yeah. You made a bet. I took it. Now you yelp."

"That wasn't a yelp… it was a threat, Starita."

Johnny didn't say "Good night." He felt hostile eyes watching him as he came past the cashier's desk… and some instinct made him glance through the plate glass before he opened the door.

A figure ducked out of sight on the sidewalk. A figure in upturned coat collar and low-pulled felt.

Johnny unbuttoned his overcoat and put his right hand where his left suspender buckle would have been if he had worn suspenders. Then he opened the door and stepped swiftly into the street.

One thin individual lounged twenty feet away by a lamp-post; he was too casual to look good. Both of his hands were in his overcoat pockets.

A hard-faced, thin-lipped person with shifty eyes and thin white hands was apparently just coming from the rear of Johnny's car.

Johnny strolled casually to the rear of the roadster. By the right rear wheel was a dark puddle. As he watched, a drop from the spring-leaf fell into the little pool... it glinted redly under the street lamp—redly like blood.

Johnny thought fast, saw a possible picture—a picture that had him square in the frame—and only one answer.

"ONLY A SMALL leak," said Johnny to the lounger. "But I guess I better phone the garage and have them take it in."

"Yeah?" The thin man chuckled sourly.

Johnny got to the plate-glass doors again without looking behind him, strolled nonchalantly through the café to the little table at the rear.

"Back again? You must like my comp'ny, Johnny."

"I do... just at the moment, Starita." He sat down, close to the Italian. "How's for taking a little ride, wop?"

Starita lifted shaggy eyebrows, scowled.

"Take that rod outta my side…. What th' hell do you think you can get away with in here?"

Johnny smiled mirthlessly.

"I can get away with one or two shots from this gun," he whispered. "And I'll give you ten seconds to make up your mind whether you want to take it here and now… or later."

Starita stood up.

"I'll have t' get my benny—"

"You'll get nothing except a slug in th' guts…. Keep walking and don't start anything… or I'll finish it."

"I'll catch my death of cold…. Can't I get my coat?"

"You'll never die of pneumonia, dago," Johnny grated. "Get out that door and make it snappy."

When they hit the sidewalk, the thin man started forward… but Starita frowned… lifted a warning hand. The thin man looked worried and glanced at the individual by the lamp-post.

"Better tell your boy friends not to make any breaks, Ciro."

Starita said something short and obscene.

"Okey… it's your funeral," said Johnny. "Now, then… climb into that car and make it fast… behind the wheel… that's it."

The thin man sauntered over close to the car.

"Don't forget you're a leaky tank there, mister. That car might blow up on you."

"This gun'll blow into *you* in about half a second, unless you stay a lot farther away," growled Johnny. "Stand clear, there."

Starita said: "You want me to drive?"

"Bright baby. Step on that starter and don't try ditching us… because if we leave the road or hit anything… you'll never wake up to find out what it was all about."

"All right, all right." The Italian got the motor going, shifted gears.

"Where're we headin' for?"

"Home, James."

"I dunno where you live, Johnny."

"Not my home... *yours*."

"What th' hell?"

"You'll find out when we get there."

Starita turned south and east, drove in silence until they pulled up before a three-story brownstone in the East Nineties. There was no one else in sight on the block.

JOHNNY GOT OUT first, held his gun waist high and said:

"Open that rumble seat, you ———!"

"What's it all about, Johnny?"

"Open that rumble seat, before I open you with a couple of .45 holes in your belly."

"Okey! Okey!"

Starita yanked on the rumble seat handle, opened it.

"Jerry!" breathed Johnny. "Gimme a chance to pull this trigger, Starita, will you?... It'd be a pleasure."

"Cripes, Johnny. How'd he get in here... all cut up that way?"

"I suppose you don't know, eh?"

"Jeeze, Johnny, you got me all wrong."

"I've got you right, baby. Now...."

"Ouch!"

"Get hold of him... lift him up.... Sure, that's it.... Carry him in... upstairs."

The Italian grunted, swore fervently; beads of sweat trickled off his swarthy nose. Johnny fished the keys out of his trousers, opened the door. They got upstairs.

"Put him on the sofa," said Johnny. Starita breathed with relief.

"You ain't gonna try to pin this on me, are ya?"

"I'm not gonna try, you louse.... I'm gonna do it."

The telephone rang. Johnny said:

"Get over there and answer that phone, you ———!"

Starita picked up the receiver. Johnny put his gun in the small of Starita's back, grabbed the receiver and whispered:

"Say 'yuh.'"

"Yuh," said Starita.

"Tell him to come right over."

"Come right over."

"Tell him you can't talk any more."

"I can't talk now.... Come ahead."

Johnny hung up.

"That was your two boy friends and they're coming over.... Will I be a reception committee!"

Starita's eyes bulged.

"It's a frame," he said.

"That's something you ought to know plenty about, dago."

"What do you want me to do?"

"March right downstairs."

"But, what th' hell—?"

"You'll find out."

They left the body of the murdered goalie on the sofa, closed the door, and went downstairs. The rumble seat was still open. A little dark red pool had gathered on the floor of the car.

"Climb in that rumble seat," said Johnny.

"You ain't gonna—?"

"Get in… or I'll throw you in."

Starita stood on the step, his beady eyes gauging the possibility of a last-minute rush. Johnny showed teeth and lifted the muzzle of his automatic.

"Come and get in, wop," he said, softly.

Ciro climbed in.

"Not that way. Lie down there, in the bottom of the car."

"Jeeze, Johnny—there ain't no room. I'll smother to death."

"That would be too good for you, Starita. But at least you'd smother yourself… and save me a lot of trouble." He lifted the butt of the heavy automatic, crashed it hard on the oily skull of the crouching figure in the car.

Starita moaned weakly, slumped to the floor. Johnny hit him again.

"I hope it didn't fracture your thick head," he murmured. He closed the rumble seat, left the car, went back into the house and waited behind the outside door.

THE BELL JANGLED wildly, rang again—shrill and startling.

Johnny stood behind the door, swung it wide.

The thin man with the fidgety fingers came first; Johnny smashed him behind the ear with the butt of his gun. The one with the low-pulled fedora and the high-turned collar saw the swift movement of the gun… backed away and reached for his hip.

"Come on in, sweetheart," gritted Johnny. "I don't want to mess up the front steps—but I'm sure going to do it if you don't come in here."

"Cripes' sake… where's Starita?"

"Come in and find out."

"Okey, okey… I'm comin'.…"

Johnny got him inside before the muzzle of the .45; locked the door and went through his pockets.

He got him into the room where Jerry's mangled body lay, let him get an eyeful and said: "Your job?"

"Nerts, wise guy. I ain't ever seen this mugg before."

"Starita says you've seen him. Says you killed him."

"Horse."

"The dago says he paid you for the job."

"Try an' prove it."

Johnny said: "No, I won't try. I won't even bother to find out."

"Well, whatcha bullin' about, then?"

"I'm going to take it for granted you did it… and let the cops prove it. Lie down on the floor."

The closed door of the room opened a fraction of an inch, noiselessly. That would be the thin punk. Johnny hadn't hit him too hard.

Johnny lifted his gun, got a line on the door-jamb and put a slug an inch from the knob.

There was a smothered curse, the sound of stumbling feet taking the stairs four at a time, the slam of a door… and finally… the purr of an eight-cylinder motor which Johnny recognized for his own.

He walked over… took a free-arm swing and put the gun-butt right between the eyes of the man in the overcoat. The latter didn't even grunt.

Johnny found the phone:

"Headquarters? Gimme th' Homicide Squad room.…

Yeah.... Say, come up to Ciro Starita's dump on East Ninety
————... I'll say there's been a murder.... Sure, still here...
sure.... Jerry Broach of the *Eagles*... all messed up.... I don't
know his name, but he's all wrapped up for you.... All you got
to do is hand him th' works and he'll squawk."

Johnny got the headquarters operator again and asked for a
radio alarm on his stolen car. He smoked three cigarettes and
answered the bell.

A couple of men from the Homicide Squad came into the
room.

"Cryin' out loud! Johnny... and playin' around with dead men
first time we find you."

"Sorry to contradict... but this wasn't my corpse. Jerry was a
good friend of mine. These babies put him on the dot because
he wouldn't fit into their picture of a hockey frameup, that's all."

"That's Slash Duter on the floor... he's out on a suspended
sentence now... gawdsake... he cut Broach up like that?"

"He and another one from the same school."

"Where's the other one?"

"The traffic B boys are all set for him to try a getaway in my
car...."

The doorbell rang again.

He let in a very disheveled individual with water dripping
from his sleeves and trousers legs... hatless and shivering...
with his long white fingers jerking convulsively. Two leath-
er-legginged, uniformed men held him.

"We got him, Johnny," said one. "But, hell! We couldn't save
your car. He drove it right off the end of the pier at a Hundred
and Fifty-seventh Street. Maybe the tugs and a derrick or so'll
be able to drag it out tomorrow."

Johnny swore. "Drove my car into the river you say! Good ————!"

"Yeah."

"Why, the lousy ————! Well, well, I hadn't figured on that. I did think he'd try a getaway… but it never occurred to me that he'd try to cover up his tracks by driving my bus into the drink."

The soaking one grinned wolfishly.

"Just a stolen car rap," he said. "That's all you got on me."

They led him upstairs, let him look at the body on the sofa.

"Holy mother of ————! Who was in that rumble seat, then?" he got out.

Johnny blew smoke into his eyes:

"Your pal, Starita."

"*Starita?* Jeeze… was *he* dead, too?"

"He wasn't," Johnny said, "until you drove him into the North River under the impression you were hiding the murder of Jerry Broach."

"You knew he was there, Johnny?" The cop was puzzled.

"Me? Sure."

"Then what in hell—why'd you let this mugg…."

"Why'd I let him run off with my car? I didn't, Sergeant. He beat it while I was busy with his pal. I was going to bring them both to the station-house. And that's what you call poetic justice. We'd never been able to pin a murder conviction on Starita. If he'd have been caught with his pal… maybe the pal would have squealed."

"I drowned him… drowned th' boss!" muttered the man. "Jeeze…."

"You lost a damn' good car, Johnny," the sergeant said dryly.

"Well, there's still thirty grand of Starita's dough I can lay my hands on…. I can clip a thousand off the roll for a new bus."

"Thirty grand! Say... who gets the rest of that roll, Johnny?"

"Jerry left a wife, Officer. I think she could use that money pretty well... and I'm going to see she gets it."

About the Author

STEWART STERLING IS the pen name of a veteran magazine editor, radio writer, and author of a staggering quantity of fiction.

Upon his graduation from Dartmouth College in 1916, where he used his bulk (225 pounds) to good purpose as left tackle on the varsity football team, he began his writing career on the staffs of various newspapers, coming to New York City in 1920 to begin a 14-year period as editor of various journals and trade publications. In 1925, he began to write pulp fiction and whodunit stories, and estimates that his work at one time or another has appeared in every pulp magazine. His radio writing began in 1932, and he has turned out since that time more than 1,500 half-hour network shows, depicting the adventures of such distinguished radio sleuths as Sherlock Holmes, Jimmy Valentine, and the heroes of *Eno Crime Clues*.

The author's interest in fire-fighting and the men who run the fire departments, which led him to write *Where There's Smoke*, is based upon a life-time study of the municipal war against two deadly enemies—fire and crime. The crime-busters, crooks, and action of the book are drawn from the dramatic happenings of real life, since the author looks with suspicion upon many of fiction's intuitive amateur detectives and fantastic criminals who, he believes, could not exist outside the pages of a book.

www.ingramcontent.com/pod-product-compliance
Lightning Source LLC
Chambersburg PA
CBHW050525260626
47157CB00004B/1474